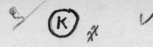

"Are you coming in for a swim?" Aaron asked

Aaron hovered like a threatening Adonis while Romy panicked. Tania wasn't supposed to be able to swim— she must remember to stay in the shallows.

"You know I don't care much for the water," Romy murmured untruthfully as she turned away to avoid his penetrating stare.

"Only because you can't swim." Aaron clearly disapproved. "With the deep water you're likely to get into, you'd better learn." His amber eyes glittered menacingly. "Come on...I'll teach you."

Romy let out a shriek and tugged against him as he hauled her down the beach. She knew she had sounded like a frightened beginner, but what she was really afraid of was the inevitable physical contact with him.

What would he do to her if he found out that she was deceiving him?

ELIZABETH POWER was once a legal secretary, but when the compulsion to write became too strong, she abandoned affidavits, wills and conveyances in favor of a literary career. Her husband, she says, is her best critic. And he's a good cook, too—often readily taking over the preparation of meals when her writing is in full flow. They live in a three-hundred-year-old English country estate cottage, surrounded by woodlands and wildlife. Who wouldn't be inspired to write?

Books by Elizabeth Power

HARLEQUIN ROMANCE
2825—RUDE AWAKENING

ELIZABETH POWER

shadow in the sun

Harlequin Books

TORONTO • NEW YORK • LONDON
AMSTERDAM • PARIS • SYDNEY • HAMBURG
STOCKHOLM • ATHENS • TOKYO • MILAN

Harlequin Presents first edition May 1988
ISBN 0-373-11078-2

Original hardcover edition published in 1987
by Mills & Boon Limited

CHAPTER ONE

FROM the plane, Romy Morgan gazed down upon the lush, green plateaux of Viti Levu, a vivid emerald against the cool, sparkling sapphire of the Pacific. During the first part of the flight from Melbourne she had knitted, read and dozed, but now the final stage of the journey to the Fijian capital had her sitting up in her seat, excitement mingling with apprehension, causing a tight knot in the pit of her stomach.

Had she been wise in coming here? Perhaps she'd been too rash, allowing herself to be talked into such a foolhardy plan.

Surreptitiously, she slipped her mirror out of her handbag, still unable to believe the reflection which stared back at her.

No one would know she was wearing contact lenses. The cornflower-blue eyes were wide and clear beneath shadowed lids. Too heavily shadowed, she thought, wryly. Just as her lipstick was a little too dark and the blusher beneath the high cheekbones far removed from the soft, natural complexion she preferred. But the idea had been to look glamorous—exactly like Tania—and with the addition of a stylish bob transforming the unmanageable fair hair, she did. So much so—she smiled to herself, replacing the mirror—that she'd had a job convincing airport officials that she was still the plain girl with glasses in her passport photograph. So what could go wrong?

'Tania! Tania Morgan!'

Romy's eyes shot open, the moment's relaxation she had been enjoying shattered by the jarring, broad Australian accent. A tall, blond man was leaning across the empty seat next to hers, looking as if he had just landed a prize catch, and Romy shrank back into her own, apprehension coiling in the pit of her stomach. Tania had said very few people here knew her *that* well, so what were the odds against meeting someone who knew her before they'd even touched down?

'Forgotten me already?' the man commented, as Romy, speechless for a few moments, grew increasingly sticky beneath the red cotton suit. 'I suppose it takes more than a newspaperman these days to impress a top TV personality.'

Meaning that with her travelogues, chat shows and host appearances, Tania's was becoming one of the most famous names on Australian television, Romy accepted, and everyone knew that her male acquaintances were usually renowned for their social standing. She released the breath she hadn't realised she had been holding. So the man thought she'd simply forgotten him, she decided, relieved, though she hadn't liked the hint of sarcasm with which he had said it.

'I'm sorry, I...'

'Oh, don't apologise.' He leaned closer, his blue eyes appearing lashless against his tan. 'I'm sure it'll come back to you. So what brings you back to Fiji...the weather? Or does it hold some greater attraction this time?'

Romy gulped, swallowing hard, not sure what he was implying. And anyway, what could she say? That Tania was supposed to spend three months a year at the house she rented on the island—though she didn't always comply—and that, just when her landlord was threatening to sell the place to an interested buyer if she failed to appear this summer, she'd landed an assignment that was too good to miss, so she had sent her twin here in her place?

Romy shuddered, involuntarily. In all of her twenty-three years she had never agreed to anything so crazy! And anyway, the man would never believe it, she thought. It wasn't common knowledge that Tania Morgan had a twin sister, and that was how Romy

wanted things to remain. Having no desire to get caught
in a publicity trap, she'd stressed, right from the start
of Tania's television career, that she wanted complete
anonymity, and her twin had always respected her decision even if she didn't seem fully to understand it.

'Would you believe sea, sun and sand?' she delivered
casu-ally to the stranger, glancing away to look out of
the window again. Rain forests were giving way to gentle
hillside—a soft contrast against the island's more rugged,
mountainous terrain—while on the horizon a chain of
smaller islands reached out—like an emerald necklace—
into the distant west.

'It wouldn't be anything to do with...' He hesitated
so that she looked at him curiously—saw him smile as
if he'd read some deadly secret in her mind before
shrugging, almost as if changing his mind about whatever
he had been going to say, to add, 'Aaron Blake?'

Blonde hair caught the sunlight as Romy shifted uncomfortably in her seat, the warm smile of a passing
hostess failing to dispel the odd shiver of foreboding the
name sent through her.

A man who was clever. '*And* dangerous,' her twin had
explained with her love for overstatement. 'Whom one
would have to be a complete idiot—or a masochist—to
try and outwit!' A property developer, Romy remembered being told, who was not only the landlord's cousin,
but also probably the only person on the island shrewd
enough to guess that she wasn't Tania.

'Why should it have anything to do with him?' she
asked the fair-haired man, wondering why her voice
shook. After all, Tania had assured her that this paragon
of shrewdness would be away all summer, but fingers
of uncertainty still tightened around Romy's stomach.

'Oh, I don't know...thought you might have a yen
for the older, more mature man.' He looked at her
obliquely. 'After all, he's still unattached. And wealthy—
unbelievably wealthy. I wouldn't mind being in his position when I'm his age!'

Through the drone of the aeroplane, Romy sensed that he was baiting her—weighing her response—and she shivered in spite of the day's heat. He was a newspaperman, she reminded herself, cautiously. Probably fishing for a new angle on Tania Morgan's love life. He wouldn't be the first. Even so, she doubted that, in spite of her sister's reputation for illustrious menfriends, Tania had yet progressed to the father-figure.

Irritated, she was about to convey something along those lines to the man in the gangway, but the sign to fasten seat-belts flashed up and he was moving away, muttering something about seeing her on the ground.

She hoped not. There was something about him she didn't like. And anyway, she had come here to write, she thought resolutely, looking forward to the perfect isolation which Tania's island home promised.

She saw him again battling through a crowd of holidaymakers at the airport—saw him gesture for her to wait for him. But, grabbing up her cases as quickly as she could, she shot off to find a cab, utterly relieved when one drew up almost immediately.

She didn't want to get too involved with anyone who knew her sister, however remotely, she thought, when the rattling vehicle was taking her through Suva's busy streets. As twins, they might *look* identical, but that was where the similarity ended, and it wouldn't take much for anyone with a modicum of intelligence to realise it at once. Tania was dazzling, flamboyant—like their mother, Romy reflected, recalling the beautiful woman who had died when they were still only eleven. And Tania needed people around her, enjoying the limelight and a whirlwind of a social life—an ever-changing circle of acquaintances. Quite unlike herself, Romy compared, favouring solitude, and the treasure of one or two longstanding friendships. But then she had always been the academic one, sharing her father's love of books and writing. Like him, she'd had a measure of success writing for children. Until now, she thought, with a sadness clouding her eyes, because since Henry Morgan's death three months ago, she hadn't written anything worth publishing—a fact Tania had pointed out to her rather insensitively in her efforts to persuade her to come here.

'I can always tell when you've got writer's block,' her twin had gone on to enlarge. 'You knit compulsively.' And with a derogatory look at Romy's busy needles, 'You knit and knit and knit but you never actually *make* anything. You need a month in Fiji,' she'd pressed with an extravagant sweep of her hand. 'That's all I'm asking, because I've been there for two months already this year, but I can't manage the third, and I'm not allowed to sublet the place so I'm going to lose it if I'm not seen to be there again this time. I don't want that to happen.'

Bracing herself as the taxi took a corner rather too sharply, Romy remembered asking her twin why keeping the house was so important to her—whether it wouldn't be best to let it go.

'You're kidding?' Identical blue eyes had met hers, aghast. 'Do you know what it's like being constantly in the spotlight? Working weekends and evenings? Getting up at dawn? Not to mention the travelling and the discomfort of some of the locations we go to. It's exhausting sometimes, particularly when one job follows another without a break. At the end of it all I need to unwind...go somewhere where I can be out of the public eye for a while, and the further the better. I need that house, Romy,' she'd added with unusual supplication, 'and you're the only person who can help me hang on to it. And who knows...' Her eyes had suddenly twinkled mischievously. 'A few weeks away could be all it takes to make you see that that dishy publisher of yours is a lot more interested in you than you realise.'

As the vehicle continued its bumpy journey through town, Romy smiled, and thought of Roger Stainsbury. Tall, good-looking and the right side of thirty, he'd been her father's publisher as well as her own, and had made no secret of the fact that his interest in her was more than just professional. An old family friend, he often took her out to lunch or dinner, or sometimes to a show, and was such good company that she could relax entirely with him. But she'd never really considered him in a more serious light...

She remembered laughing aside Tania's remarks, more concerned with how tired her sister had looked beneath the heavy make-up. Partly through overworking, Romy had suspected, although she'd guessed, too, that her twin was mourning the father she'd never really seen eye to eye with, more than she was prepared to admit, and she'd known then that she would have to help her out. After all, they had always been close, particularly as children, Romy reflected now, even if in recent years their diverse life-styles had seemed to pull them apart. And there *had* been odd occasions when one had stood in for the other, she reminded herself, trying to dispel doubts. Like that last-minute substitution on that casual date, those nerve-racking speeches at college, and before that, at school, when, favouring the other's lessons, they had prankishly 'switched' classes. But whether she could keep up a pretence for a whole month she had yet to discover, only now ready to accept that her sister had been right. She, herself, *had* needed to get away.

Her father's death had hit her hard and, with Tania owning her own apartment in the more expensive part of town, the huge house had seemed too lonely, so that sometimes Romy's own loss had been almost too much to bear. And with no other relatives—since both their parents had been only children—her crushing need to strengthen her relationship with her sister had helped to cement her decision.

Consequently, within two weeks she had put the house on the market, had her hair cut, and with a few professional tips on make-up from Tania, found herself here in Fiji.

Now she was glad she had, she thought, looking out of the car window, her apprehension melting under the high, tropical sun.

They had left the bustling town behind them, old colonial and modern architecture giving way to coconut palms, mangrove and other lush green vegetation. Rivers flowed down from the distant hills—twisting ribbons of silver in the sunlight—while away to the right, the deep blue of the Pacific seemed to stretch for ever like a glittering jewel.

And suddenly—unexpectedly—they were there, turning off a dusty hillside track into a belt of trees, the one-storey house being exactly as Tania had described, it with a long, sloping roof and a veranda leading all the way round from the front steps.

'Niki will be expecting you...or rather...*me*,' Tania had told her impishly, 'but normally she's only there mornings so you won't have to worry too much about her.'

Which was just as well, Romy thought now, flushing guiltily as the slim, young native girl came up to her as she was climbing out of the taxi and politely asked if Miss Morgan had had a good trip.

'It wasn't bad.' Romy applied some of Tania's cool indifference to her voice as Niki led her inside, an interior graced with modern cane and wicker furniture which complemented perfectly the Persian rugs and tapestries adorning the floors and walls.

'It's lovely!' She couldn't keep the thrill out of her voice as she looked around her. Then she saw Niki frowning and realised that she was supposed to have been here countless times before, so she added quickly, 'As always.'

Phew! she thought, unsettled, only then realising how careful she would need to be to carry this thing off. I'm going to have to watch *every* word.

Grateful when Niki smilingly suggested that she might like to freshen up before tea, Romy thanked her and, after finding the bedroom from Tania's precise instructions, peeled off her cotton suit and blouse and went through into the shower.

When she came back into the bedroom in a gaily coloured caftan, Niki was unpacking the last of her belongings.

'Thanks, but I could have done that.'

Towelling the short, blonde hair, Romy instantly grasped that she had said the wrong thing. Tania would have taken being waited on as a matter of course. And, feeling awkward when the girl made no comment, she strode over to the window.

Way up on the hill, nestling amid the trees, she could see a much larger house with a flat, terraced roof, its closed windows glinting in the afternoon sun. Scarlet hibiscus and bougainvillaea lent splashes of vibrant colour to its austere white walls, while treeferns, bamboo and yaka trees bowed towards it in the warm wind.

'Mr Blake...he's still away.'

Niki was behind her, brown eyes following cornflower blue in the direction of the mini-mansion, her short curly hair as black as ebony.

'Yes...yes, I know,' said Romy, gulping, startled to learn that this wealthy, middle-aged businessman lived so close. This house was practically on his doorstep! Although Tania had forgotten to mention that. Perhaps she'd thought it unnecessary, Romy decided, since he was going to be absent all summer.

'Redesigning Adelaide,' was how her twin had so elaborately put it.

Nevertheless, she still couldn't help the nervous contraction of her throat, and wondered why even his huge, empty house should seem intimidating.

'He was very angry that last night, wasn't he?' Niki's voice cracked slightly, and there was a soft tinge of colour on the dusky skin. 'I'd never seen him in such a temper.'

With you? Romy nearly asked, then stopped herself. She was supposed to be Tania, wasn't she? Therefore she would probably know. But the thought of anyone as shrewd as this Aaron Blake being around wasn't doing a great deal for her nerves, and determinedly she had to force it to the back of her mind. The man was away, wasn't he? she told herself firmly, guessing that it was only guilt which was making her so uneasy, so that by the time she went to bed that night she had managed to convince herself that she had nothing to worry about.

When she got up the next morning Niki had already been in and gone out again, because there was a tray in the kitchen set for breakfast. A jug of orange juice and a bowl of fruit—pawpaw, pineapple and grapefruit—and there was freshly baked bread, too. Still in her cotton négligé, Romy made some coffee and took the tray outside on to the veranda. The sea was a lazy murmur against the livelier sounds of the morning: a parrot shrieking intermittently from an acacia tree nearby; the high whine of a speedboat engine some way out at sea; a bee drowning lazily over the frangipani.

She could have sat there for hours. But she had come here to work, she reminded herself firmly and, summoning up all the will-power she could find, she eventually dragged herself inside, showering again before pulling on jeans and a pale blue sun-top and securing the short, blonde hair behind her ears with slides.

Coming out of the bathroom, she stopped dead, her gaze going to the open door to the veranda.

He was standing there in the aperture—a tall, powerfully built figure blocking out the sun. Well over six feet, Romy deduced, swallowing, feeling dwarfed even at her own five feet nine inches. Dark hair—glinting red in the sun—crowned strong, arresting features: a high forehead above a long, straight nose, thick brows and clear, amber eyes, while the firm, commanding mouth which sealed his air of authority smiled down at her perplexed face with humourless mockery.

'Shocked, Tania?' A deep, resonant baritone which sent odd warning signals along her spine.

Nervously, she licked her lips, swallowing again, hard. And only then realised that she was trembling.

Who on earth was he? she wondered, frantically. Tania hadn't mentioned a man about thirty-six who was a cross between a bronze Adonis and a tower of granite! But he seemed to know *her*!

'Well...aren't you going to ask me in?' A tone which was cool—half derisive—and which called upon a primeval instinct in her for self-protection.

'Of—of course.'

She sounded like a stammering adolescent, she thought, stepping back instinctively as he entered.

His presence dominated the little place, she noted with an odd shiver; noted, too, how the casual blue shirt and light trousers did little to conceal the muscular lines of broad shoulders and firm, powerful thighs.

'I must admit you're as much a surprise to me as I am to you,' he drawled, mockery in the deep tones again, as the cool, amber eyes studied her with a piercing scrutiny. 'I hardly recognised you without your make-up.'

Her make-up! Involuntarily, Romy's hands flew to her cheeks. Of course! Tania never allowed herself to be seen by anyone before she had put her 'face' on! Thank goodness she'd at least put her new lenses in when she'd got up, instead of reverting to her glasses as she'd been tempted to, thinking she'd be alone!

'I was just about to put some on,' she prevaricated, inwardly annoyed with her sister for not even bothering to warn her about this man. Was he a boyfriend? she wondered, disorderedly. And if so, to what degree?

Shaken by the conjecture, she half turned, blabbering some wild excuse about making herself more presentable, but with startling reflexes he brought strong fingers around her wrist, and warning signals leaped in her again as the hand tightened cruelly on the soft flesh, making her wince—her pulse race.

'No, don't bother.' His tone was as commanding as the hard line of his mouth. 'I prefer you like this for once. You look much more...vulnerable.'

A word laced with sensual mockery which brought her red-tipped fingers splaying against his chest in sudden panic as she came up hard against him. Half afraid—half annoyed, she pushed against the broad wall of his chest, and a small guttural sound escaped her when she realised that it was useless.

'Yes... I like you like this.' He had caught her hair at the nape of her neck, making her gasp as he tugged her head back so that the slim, patrician features were open to his cold regard. 'It gives a man chance to see the real Tania Morgan.'

If only he knew! she thought, gulping, under no illusion that he actually preferred the way *she* looked to her more glamorous twin. She'd learned from experience that when men who knew she was Tania's sister showed any interest in *her*, it was usually in the hope of a subsequent introduction to her twin. So what this man probably liked was her supposed vulnerability—catching her at a disadvantage. And she guessed he was a man who liked to command every situation.

He was looking at her from beneath thick, dark lashes, his hard gaze fixed on the trembling fullness of her lips, and for one hazy moment she thought that he was going to kiss her—cruelly, humiliatingly for some reason—and she tensed, the almost erotic scent of his cologne stripping her of her defences, immobilising her as she anticipated the assault of that hard mouth.

But it didn't come. Instead, his thumb brushed lightly across her lips, the action so sensual—so disturbingly different from what she had been expecting—that she could only look up at him with startled blue eyes.

'Such mock innocence,' he remarked, surprisingly gently, though his smile was without warmth. 'A pity discrimination can't be added to your list of virtues.'

'Let me go!' Anger lent her strength to pull away, and she heard him laugh softly.

'What's wrong, Tania? Am I hitting below the belt?' And when she didn't answer, too shaken for a moment to say anything, he commented, 'No instantaneous retort?' looking at her obliquely, one eyebrow raised—black against the tanned velvet of his skin. 'That isn't like you.'

Because I'm not Tania! she was all for screaming at him, her self-possession totally in shreds. Oh God, who was he? she thought, desperately. And why did he seem to despise her twin so much?

Taking her courage in both hands, somehow she managed to say, 'I came here to relax . . . not to involve myself in a sparring match with you. Or anyone else for that matter,' she added, remarkably calmly, hoping he wouldn't notice how much he was unnerving her. After all, she had come here as a favour to Tania—and to try and finish a book—and she wasn't going to throw everything to the winds just because a man had caught her totally off guard. Even if he was the most sexually disturbing man she had ever come across!

'Anyway . . .' She shrugged casually, saying with an affected little laugh—a facsimile of her twin's, 'H-how long has it been?'

Goodness, that sounded awful! But she had to say *something*—anything!—to try and find out who he was. And she could scarcely ask him outright!

'You know very well.'

Hardly an informative answer. Just that simmering anger which assured her now that here was no besotted admirer of Tania's, but more a threatening opponent whom, she, herself, would be wise not to tangle with. Even so, the lift of her head was unintentionally challenging as, feeling her way carefully, she found enough composure to say, 'I thought *you* might have forgotten.'

He moved a step nearer so that imperceptibly she flinched, aware of the power in him—the latent strength—and nervously she licked her lips. What was she thinking of . . . playing this dangerous game with a man she didn't even know? And one so threateningly male?

'I haven't forgotten,' he said, quietly, his voice rich, distinctive, its intonations allowing her to guess that he came from some part of New Zealand. 'But I didn't call to talk about last time . . . and I was more than certain you wouldn't want to. I came down simply to say,

welcome back, and since we have to live right next door
to each other, let's try and do so on more amicable terms
this time.'

Right next door! Romy's head came up so fast she
almost caught him on the chin, the colour draining out
of her cheeks as if someone had pulled some deep, inner
plug.

Of course! She should have realised! That air of wealth
he seemed to exude. That hard maturity. No one had
said the man was middle-aged, she thought, chaotically,
looking back. Not Tania. Not that reporter on the plane.
She'd only imagined that herself! And she had to stifle
the short, hysterical laugh which rose in her throat.

Every nerve tensing, she took a step back, her brain
screaming through a whirlpool of total panic that she
had come face to face with Aaron Blake!

On impulse she might have fled, but her promise to
protect her sister's tenancy held her exactly where she
stood.

'I—I thought you were going to be away all summer,'
she stammered, the hammering of her heart making her
decidedly weak. 'Why have you come back?'

Well, wasn't that what Tania would have immediately
asked? she thought wildly.

The broad shoulders lifted beneath the soft, blue shirt,
the cool amber eyes unsmiling as he said, 'To keep an
eye on you?'

Romy laughed, because that's what Tania would have
done, but more because she felt she would have col-
lapsed into a trembling pool of jelly if she didn't.

'Do I need keeping an eye on ... *Mr* Blake?' she responded cautiously, using the prefix with deliberate emphasis because she wasn't sure how to address him.
However, the cynical lift of a thick eyebrow had her
guessing that her cold formality piqued.

So her sister called him Aaron. For some reason she
found the thought most unsettling.

He hadn't answered her question, but was glancing
around at the wall tapestries and the expensive orna-

ments her twin loved to collect, and with dismay she
realised that she had forgotten to put her knitting away
last night and it was still lying on one of the wicker chairs.

She caught her breath. Tania wouldn't have been seen
dead doing anything so mundane!

Frantic to distract him, she remembered where Tania
had said he was supposed to be this summer and throwing
out her arms demonstratively, uttered, with a nervous
little laugh, 'Well...how was Adelaide?'

Immediately the man's eyes were on the thrust of her
breasts—braless beneath the blue sun-top and, disconcerted, Romy wished she hadn't drawn such obvious attention to herself. She didn't have Tania's gift for being
flamboyant.

'It was busy,' he said, answering her. 'It was
noisy...overcrowded to the point of being claustro-
phobic...and I missed the islands.' This with a hint of
quiet sentiment which surprised her coming from such
an obviously hard-headed character. 'Everything was
running smoothly enough without me so I decided to
come back here.' His mouth pulled down at one corner.
'And actually, darling...it was Sydney. You should have
remembered that.'

Another mistake! Like the make-up, she thought,
gulping, feeling herself grow hot under those cool, as-
sessing eyes. She would never be able to go through with
this ridiculous pretence now.

'Are you all right?'

The hard, dark features were studying her puzzlingly,
and Romy's throat constricted. He could probably see
the beads of perspiration breaking out above her top lip!
she thought wryly, but hung on to enough composure
to respond surprisingly casually, 'Of course I am. Why?'

Fortunately, footsteps outside distracted him and he
was greeting Niki who came in with her arms laden with
groceries. She coloured when Aaron spoke to her, ad-
dressing him as '*Turaga*', and Romy suddenly realised
the amount of respect he would command. She wondered how accurate Tania's assessment of him had been

when she'd said one would have to be a complete fool to try and outwit him. Deadly so, she suspected, shuddering, knowing that if she stayed here, that was exactly what she would have to do.

He said something she didn't catch, but which made Niki laugh and blush more profusely before she turned and padded barefoot into the kitchen.

'Did you know your loyal little maid has got herself betrothed to my handyman?' The strong chin lifted in the direction the girl had gone. 'I think she'll probably prefer to help Raku up at the house when they're married, so you could be losing her shortly.'

'Meaning she'll be working for you instead?'

It was a simple enough question—uttered hastily for something to say. So why had it come out almost as an accusation? Because of the need to defend herself against this man?

A spark of antagonism flickered in the amber eyes. 'Would that annoy you, Tania?' He was taking in the creamy softness of her shoulders, the swell of her breasts and the length of her denim-clad legs, enjoying a leisurely tour of her body right down to her red-tipped toes in the thonged sandals, and Romy felt hot colour steal across her skin.

'Why should it?' she countered, embarrassment making her tone acrid. His lazy, sensual appraisal of her was far too disturbing for comfort!

He shrugged, his eyes returning to her face and its telltale colour, and a line deepened between the black brows.

'Are you *sure* you're all right?'

Romy swallowed, steadying herself. 'Of course.' God, she had to get rid of him, and soon! Before he guessed the truth! Tania wouldn't have blushed just because a man looked at her. Neither would you normally, she admitted to herself. Only Aaron Blake wasn't your average kind of man. Neither was this an average kind of situation!

'It's rather unsettling for a girl to be caught looking like this,' she bluffed, tilting her chin to draw attention

to her lack of make-up and hoping he'd assume that that
was why she was so edgy. 'Do you think you could come
back when I've made myself a bit more presentable?'
She only had the courage to suggest it because she had
no intention of staying here any longer than she could
help. As soon as he was gone she was going to telephone
Tania and tell her that she couldn't possibly go ahead
with this hare-brained plan. There was still time. She
could leave instantly—within the next hour if possible—
and Tania would have to sort out her tenancy problems
for herself.

'Feminine pride?' Aaron's words were softly mocking,
but he *was* complying—moving towards the door—and
Romy stifled a sigh of relief. 'Be seeing you,' he said
coolly, with a last, unnerving glance at her before he
went.

'That's what you think!' she muttered when he was
out of earshot. She wasn't staying around here another
minute!

Darting into the bedroom, she started dialling Tania's
apartment, choosing the extension so that Niki wouldn't
overhear. There was no reply though, and after some
difficulty she managed to get through to the television
studios where her sister worked, biting her lower lip as
someone answered.

'I'm sorry...everyone connected with the safari assignment has already left,' a smooth, feminine voice announced in reply to Romy's urgent question, 'and
no...I'm afraid I don't have a number where they can
be reached.'

Her heart sinking, Romy thanked the woman,
dropping the telephone back on to its cradle.

It couldn't be possible! she thought, dismayed. She
must have missed her sister by hours, and now Tania
would be somewhere in the middle of Africa for the next
month, so there wasn't any chance of contacting her
again. What could she do?

Agitatedly, she paced the room chewing on her bottom
lip. She couldn't just drop everything and leave—that

would be unfair to her twin. But how was she going to keep up this pretence with a man like Aaron Blake around?

Outside a bird shrieked in alarm to another, and uneasily Romy paused by the window, her gaze following the track the man must have taken to reach the impressive white house, her mind in a turmoil.

He was totally male—hard and shrewd—and it wouldn't take much for a man like that to see right through this little charade, she thought, shuddering, wishing she'd followed her initial instinct and refused when Tania had asked her to come here. At least when she'd agreed to, she hadn't reckoned on an entanglement with the landlord's dominating cousin, and gnawing at her too was the disturbing question of what sort of relationship her sister had with him. She remembered the reporter on the plane intimating that the association might be more than neighbourly, and now she knew why. She had looked glamorous, and Aaron Blake was an attractive and extremely virile man. Glamorous women would probably play a very active role in his life. He had called her 'darling', too, she reflected, perturbed. But was that just a casual term he used to address any reasonably attractive woman? Or did it have hidden connotations?

She shuddered again, dreading to think. Surely Tania would have told her if she'd been romantically involved with a man like that? They'd never had any secrets from each other. And reluctant though she was to admit it, she couldn't deny that Aaron Blake would be a feather in any girl's cap.

I'm just building things up, she thought admonishingly, strolling out into the garden in an attempt to ease her worries.

The air was sweet—redolent with frangipani, the startling reds of the bougainvillaea as striking as the ocean was blue.

This place was paradise. But could she stay here and keep Aaron from guessing that she wasn't her twin? Because when Niki had mentioned seeing him lose his temper, she knew now that it had been with Tania, not the servant girl as she'd first thought. And that anger was still there—for whatever reason—behind that mocking smile, in those beautiful amber eyes. And as long as she was here posing as Tania, Romy knew that she was going to be the one to feel the sting of it.

CHAPTER TWO

AARON BLAKE had flown to Lautoka on business, Niki told Romy the following morning, which explained why he hadn't put in any further appearances. She wondered where the servant girl obtained her information, deciding that it was probably from Aaron's handyman—Niki's fiancé, she remembered him saying—and was relieved, therefore, that she could at least work without any fear of him turning up.

But a lack of inspiration combined with the tense state she'd been in since meeting him yesterday wasn't conducive to good writing, and consequently, after breakfast, she ambled down to the beach.

It was a long stretch of white sand, palm-shaded and deserted, and the blue ocean looked so inviting that immediately she was discarding her jeans and cotton top, and wading in.

The water was warm, breaking over her lemon bikini like a gentle caress, and with an exhilarating sense of freedom Romy kicked away from the shore, her ability as a confident swimmer showing itself in the agility and grace of her slender body.

She was relaxing—floating on her back—when she heard the distant growl of a car engine. A red Ferrari was throwing up a cloud of dust as it headed beach-wards from the direction of the big house, and some deep-rooted instinct for self-survival warned her that it was Aaron Blake at the wheel. He was obviously back earlier than expected and had probably come down to the house to see her—or rather, Tania, she thought, instantly uneasy—and Niki must have told him that she would be down here.

23

And suddenly panic struck. Tania couldn't swim! Not with any degree of confidence anyway! And with her heart pounding in her ears, Romy struck out for the beach in a forceful front crawl, flopping down on to the brightly coloured beach towel and replacing her lenses just before the man came looming above her.

'I see you've decided to get your bikini wet this morning. Coming back in?'

'No,' she answered decisively, shielding her eyes from the sun with scarlet-tipped fingers as she tilted her head to look at him.

He was already unfastening his denim shirt, removing it to reveal a mat of dark, wiry hair and powerful shoulders. Lying at his feet, Romy swallowed, thinking him bigger than she remembered. His eyes were moving over the soft rise of her breasts, down over her waist and the plane of her stomach with obvious enjoyment and she glanced away, disconcerted, as he moved to deal with the belt of his jeans.

'Did Niki tell you where I was?' The question seemed totally unnecessary, but she needed something to say to break the tug of a physical attraction so strong that it left her weak, slightly nonplussed.

'No,' he surprised her by answering, and when she looked at him questioningly, 'Don't you always spend every morning of your first few days here on the beach?'

Romy caught her breath. Well, at least she hadn't broken with tradition, she thought, with a small sigh of relief.

'Well...are you coming in?'

She glanced up at him again from under her water-proof mascara—a prime specimen of perfect masculinity. His body was a deep bronze, biceps beautifully contoured against a broad, muscular chest. His waist and hips were narrow above powerful, hair-covered thighs, and all he was wearing now was a pair of minuscule white trunks.

'You know Tania Morgan doesn't care much for the water,' Romy murmured, truthfully, the aqua-blue shadow shimmering on her lids as she turned away from him, this strange excitement she felt from just looking at a man, a new and unsettling experience.

'Only because she never does anything more than paddle.' He clearly disapproved. 'And with the deep water you're likely to get yourself into you're going to need to be able to swim. Come on . . . I'll teach you.'

Before she could assimilate his words—wonder at the cutting edge which had crept into his voice—he grabbed her hand and she let out a shriek, tugging against him as he hauled her off the towel and started pulling her down the beach.

I must sound like a frightened beginner, she thought, hectically, when what she was really afraid of was the inevitable physical contact with him, coupled with the gnawing worry of what he might do to her if he found out that she was deceiving him.

'No, let me go!'

He laughed, ignoring her protests, and at the water's edge, swung her up into his arms.

'Now just relax,' she heard him quietly advising. But she couldn't, because the warmth of those strong arms around her back and under her knees were sending a whole host of strange sensations through her.

'Let me go,' she appealed somewhat shakily this time, and he laughed again.

'What . . . drop you here?'

They were in waist-deep water, and when Aaron suddenly dipped his arm as if to tip her head-first, she made a swift grab for him somewhere around his middle.

'You wouldn't!' she exhaled, feigning a degree of anxiety, although somehow she sensed that, had she been the beginner he really thought she was, she'd have felt quite secure in those powerful arms.

'I might,' he promised, amber eyes glittering hard. 'If you prove to be a too intractable pupil.' But it was there again—the antagonism—beneath the laughter, so that Romy tensed, and realising that her arm was still around his middle, quickly she let it fall. What *was* his relationship with Tania? she wondered, worriedly. And why did he sound so contemptuous towards her?

'Now if we start like this...'

She didn't have chance to dwell on the subject because he was lowering her face downwards on to the water, his arms like bronze bars under her body. 'Now keep your head up and kick...'

'Like this?' she queried, trying to sound uncertain, and began a violent movement with her legs which she knew was totally wrong.

'No, no. You'll splash everybody within fifty yards if you carry on like that...keep your legs together...'

He was a good teacher, or would have been had she been in need of instruction, she thought—patient, understanding a beginner's fear—but she was so aware of that wet, muscular body so close to hers, those sure, steady hands beneath her, that it was difficult enough remembering she was supposed to be Tania, without having to concentrate on pretending not to know what she was doing. And then there was the dread of being found out...

'That's right. Now here...catch hold of my hands and kick and I'll start moving back into deeper water. Feel the buoyancy lifting you?'

She did, but she could have told him about that, anyway. I could probably swim circles round him...or at least save his life if I had to, she thought with a pang of raging guilt, and suddenly realised that she wasn't enjoying this at all. Deceiving by saying nothing was almost as bad as telling blatant untruths, and desperately she wished that she had never got herself into this mess.

'My back's burning...can we go back now?' It was partly true. She had fair skin which she had to watch in the sun, but it was also the only feeble excuse she could think of to get away from him.

Aaron smirked, tossing back damp, dark hair. 'Had enough? All right...come along.'

Disconcertingly, he caught her up in his arms again and waded with her back to dry land, totally unaware of how his closeness was making her pulses race, her blood pump through her.

'Here...let me do that,' he said, when she dropped down on to the towel with a tube of sun-soother in her hand.

Romy hesitated, not wanting him to touch her again She couldn't think straight when he did, and one thing she had to do while he was around was keep her wits about her. Just one mistake on her part could cost her twin her holiday home, and she *had* come here to see that that didn't happen.

'No, that's OK.'

'Don't be stubborn,' he admonished, his tone insistent. Taking the tube from her, he unscrewed the top and squeezed a liberal portion of cream into his palm. 'Turn over.'

His peremptory command had her lying face downwards, the fine, short hair gold against the curve of her bent arm as he applied the soothing balm to her back. It was cool, his touch, oddly relaxing, and a brief contentment filled her. The surge of the ocean was relaxing, too. A rush of wind lifted the palms. And somewhere inland a dog barked hysterically, the sound muted and faint, carried to them on the warm breeze.

Romy stirred, changing arms, a small, audible sigh escaping her. Her back was slightly sore, but those hands were gentle, moving skilfully over her sensitive skin to the narrow line of her waist and the smooth curve of her hips, hands which were firm and manipulating, and which would probably know how to arouse and give pleasure...

She sat up quickly, the shock of her unbidden thoughts shattering her inner peace. He was someone she had begun a dangerous game with—not a lover! Nor did she want him to be.

'That's fine,' she said, falteringly. 'Thanks.'

He accepted her decision, tossing the tube down on to the towel before stretching out beside her, propping himself up on his elbows.

'It's been three months, hasn't it, Tania?' he remarked sombrely. 'How have you been?'

Her casual shrug hid a sudden sharp bout of apprehension. 'Fine.'

Careful, she warned herself. Don't let him unsettle you. One slip and both Tania and you could well be heading for trouble.

'How's work?'

Romy lifted blue-tinted lids to meet his eyes, the long fringes of her lashes, feathery shadows against her skin. 'Fine,' she said again.

A thick, black eyebrow lifted curiously. 'You aren't exactly loquacious this morning, are you?' he expressed, frowning, his gaze moving down over her semi-naked body as if he knew it intimately. Heat prickled along her skin and she looked away so that he wouldn't see the rise of colour in her cheeks.

Of course! She had to be much more talkative if she wanted to keep him believing she was Tania. It was not like her twin to be lost for words. Yet she hated having to lie.

'A new travel series, and a live morning chat show coming up,' she stated abruptly as a way around it. After all, she hadn't actually said *she'd* done the travelogues or was hosting the chat show. 'Oh, and a one-off half-an-hour thing on cultural marriage rites,' she added, remembering the most recent programme Tania had narrated.

'And has that helped to change your mind about being a bride?'

Was that some sort of proposal? She looked at him quickly, a soft wisp of hair blowing across her cheek. There was a hard gleam in his eyes, a derisive twist to the firm mouth which assured her at once that he was only mocking her.

'I'm not ready for marriage yet,' she answered with the stock-phrase she'd heard her sister use in various interviews, and above the lazy wash of the ocean she caught Aaron's sharp, indrawn breath.

'You mean you prefer to leave that to those naïve enough to be loyal and trusting until death. Or until something less flattering makes a complete mockery of that trust.'

God, he was cynical! Romy turned questioning blue eyes to those which were as cold and clear as amber glass and she shivered, feeling the anger in them, in the grim set of his lips—feeling it directed against *her* because he thought she was Tania. But why? Why was he so angry with her sister? she wondered, baffled. Had Tania offended him personally in some way?

'I didn't mean that at all,' she returned, stiffly, nettled by his attitude towards her twin. And flinched as he suddenly brushed the stray gold strand from her cheek, his fingers accidentally touching her lips.

'What's wrong, Tania... afraid of me?'

His voice had softened, willing her gaze to the lucid amber of his, and she met it levelly, trying not to let him see how much his touch had affected her.

'Of course not,' she answered, lifting her small chin in rebellion, battling against an urge to run back up the beach and as far away from this man and this absurd situation as she could possibly get.

'Then why did you leave so hurriedly last time?' The strong, dark features studied hers intently. 'Was it seeing the worst side of my anger? Or did you decide that leaving that way was the best way of avoiding adverse publicity?'

What on earth was he talking about? Her brow furrowed slightly. What kind of publicity would Tania have needed to avoid?

Uneasily, Romy dropped her gaze to the line of dark hair that ran down his abdomen into the brief, white trunks, noticing the beads of water still glistening against the hard, bronzed thighs. She touched her tongue to her lips, searching desperately for something to say which wouldn't betray her as an impostor, when a shout cut through the tension between them, granting her a welcome reprieve.

'Hold it!'

With a small cry Romy turned away as a camera shutter started clicking ominously. She heard Aaron swear under his breath and the next moment saw him springing to his feet.

'Get out of here, Swain, if you value your job! This is a private stretch of beach.'

Romy instantly recognised the reporter from the plane, although he looked different now in cut-off jeans and a gaping check shirt. Seeing Aaron's savage expression he had stopped dead in his tracks—tall and blond and tanned, yet looking strangely insipid, Romy thought, against the other man's dark attraction.

'I'm only a hard-working guy trying to earn a living, and all I want is a few photographs of Australia's favourite celebrity.' He tossed a glance in Romy's direction. 'Nothing wrong with that, is there?'

'Miss Morgan's on holiday and doesn't want to be photographed,' Aaron growled, so vehemently that the reporter took a step back. But he wasn't easily intimidated.

'That's only your opinion...can't the little lady speak for herself?' He glanced towards her again, his mouth twisting unpleasantly. 'Or perhaps I'll get more co-operation elsewhere.' The camera was lifted again. 'Like from a certain offic...'

Suddenly, Aaron was lunging forward—grabbing the camera—and a moment later a coil of expensive film was being tossed into the sand.

'Hey? What the...'

'I told you to get out of here.' Aaron's voice was thick with loathing and he looked very much as if he would have liked to have hit the man, Romy thought, as she saw him thrust the camera back into its owner's hands.

'All right, all right! I'm going.'

Scowling, the reporter backed away, muttering something under his breath before turning and virtually running back along the sand.

'Wasn't that a bit excessive?' Romy suggested, shakily. She knew this sort of thing happened to her sister quite often—over-zealous newspapermen wanting photographs or any news items that they could get about her. But it was Aaron's reaction to it that had brought her out in goose-pimples. His anger had been positively explosive.

'I hardly think so.' Glowering darkly, he picked up the denim shirt and shrugged into it, fastening several studs. 'They're all the same—the Press. And he's the lowest.'

Surprise lit Romy's eyes. 'For wanting a picture?' She said it without thinking—wished she could retract it when she saw the odd way he was looking at her—but she couldn't understand why his temper had flared like that.

His mouth pulled down grimly at one corner. 'He wants more than a picture, my dear child, and you know it,' he delivered scathingly, fastening his belt.

So the man wanted a story about Tania as well, Romy thought with a mental shrug. What harm was there in that? She frowned, thinking back to what Aaron had said earlier about Tania wanting to avoid adverse publicity, and the line deepened between her eyes. Publicity about what? she wondered, worriedly. And did that have something to do with that man Swain?

'Goodness knows how he found out you were back,' Aaron exhaled, raking his fingers through the dark, springy hair, and Romy pressed her lips together, thinking this time before she spoke.

'We were on the same plane.' At least she could safely say that, she decided exasperatedly, finding this deception becoming more of a strain by the second. 'He would have liked an interview then, but I didn't give him the chance.' Now that sounded more like the confident twin who was used to dealing with the Press.

'Come on.' Aaron's hand was on her arm, hauling her to her feet, his fingers biting hard into the soft flesh.

'Where are we going?' she asked, half annoyed at the way he was suddenly ordering her around—wincing from the bruising pressure of his grip.

'Well, *you're* going back to the house.'

'But I . . .'

'No buts,' he said firmly, dispelling all argument when he scooped up her beach towel, sandals and bag, while Romy struggled into her jeans and sun-top, utterly flabbergasted. Who did he think he was, pushing her around like this?

Obviously he thought he had every right to, because he went on, his voice deep and decisive, 'I think it best that you don't come down here on your own with that scandalmonger lurking about . . . so if you want to practise your swimming from now on I suggest you use my pool.'

She couldn't believe what he was saying as he handed her into the Ferrari. She wasn't used to possessive men trying to take charge of her life, and she doubted if Tania would have welcomed it, either.

'You don't own me, Aaron Blake,' she announced for herself and her twin, the slim, patrician features indignant within a frame of damp, gold hair.

'More's the pity,' he said roughly, noting the mutinous line of her lips as he thrust the car into gear. 'If I did, I'd have curbed that wilful behaviour of yours long before now.'

'Then it's just as well you don't, isn't it?' she was quick to retort, finding his dominating attitude infuriating even though she knew his remarks weren't really directed at her.

So her sister was wilful, she mused, when Aaron's lack of response plunged them into silence. But hadn't she always known that? It was that wilfulness, coupled with a craving for excitement, which had made Tania a wayward and unpopular teenager with their father, Romy recalled, although conversely it had also probably contributed to making her as successful as she was now.

And as the powerful car growled up the hill, Romy wondered how her twin would have handled the situation on the beach today. Certainly without turning green and breaking out in goose-pimples! She was certain of that. It would hardly be the first time that men had nearly come to blows over Tania, she thought, wondering what it would be like to have that degree of mystique—that charisma—which attracted men to her sister. Perhaps sometimes it would make life too complicated...

'You didn't answer my question.'

Aaron's sudden comment shook her. They had reached Tania's house and he was cutting the engine.

'Y-your question?' Romy faltered, confused. She hadn't realised he'd asked one.

'About why you left last time without a word.' He turned to face her, the warm seat leather squeaking beneath his weight, and Romy caught her breath, fidgeting uneasily.

God, what was she supposed to say? How was she supposed to know why Tania had left hurriedly last time—what she had done to earn this man's obvious contempt? She didn't even know if their relationship was purely neighbourly or...

She cast her tongue over her lips, dreading to think of the difficult problems she could be heading for if her sister's involvement with Aaron was more than just platonic, but bravely she lifted her chin, exposing the perfect column of her throat as she said, 'I thought we weren't going to talk about last time.'

Fortunately, her seemingly casual reminder worked. His eyes darkened momentarily, and then he tilted his head in acknowledgement—a subtle apology, the only kind, she suspected, any woman would be likely to get from him.

'Have lunch with me,' he said, suddenly, catching her completely off guard.

'I can't.'

He looked at her sceptically, the breeze from the open window gently ruffling his hair. 'Why not?'

Why couldn't she? Romy thought quickly, her gaze fixed on a small, white sail which was dipping and rising way off on the sparkling blue water.

'I'm going into Suva,' she invented, and knew she would have to now, otherwise he'd probably be shrewd enough to know about it if she didn't. But it was preferable to do that than spend any more time than she had to in his company, because she couldn't deny that she was dangerously attracted to him and she couldn't risk losing her cool—being found out.

Even so, she was rather surprised when he merely shrugged. 'Suit yourself.' He sounded almost bored. Then he was getting out and opening her door for her, his closeness so disturbing that she made a complete fool of herself as she clambered out by dropping one of the sandals she hadn't bothered to put on.

He retrieved it for her, looking mockingly down at her flushed cheeks as if he knew how aware of him she was— how alive to that masculine scent, mingling with the ocean salt on his skin.

'Remember,' she heard him warn behind her as she started towards the steps, 'if Swain comes snooping around, give me a ring. Or tell Raku if I'm not in.'

And then he was driving away, leaving Romy annoyed and more than a little confused.

Just what right did he think he had, ordering her around like this? she thought, irritated, as she slipped her feet into the sandals and strolled up past the acacia tree. And what really was the reason for the way he had lost his temper with that reporter?

Startlingly, it occurred to her as she let herself into the house that his objection to Tania being photographed might stem from a reluctance to share her with anyone else, but Romy immediately dismissed that idea as ludicrous. Somehow Aaron Blake didn't strike her as the type of man who would let a woman get under his skin to that degree. Besides, he'd done nothing to suggest that he and Tania were involved emotionally. She hadn't exactly had to fight off his advances today, had she? she thought, colour suffusing her cheeks from remembering the feel of his hands when he'd been rubbing the cream into her back—almost imagining it a lover's touch.

Well, in future she'd be on her guard against wild fantasies like that, she told herself firmly, going in to shower. She might be here as the glamorous Tania, but behind the make-up she was still Romy Morgan, and such devastating men as Aaron Blake didn't fall for ordinary, academic-type girls like herself.

Romy spent the afternoon browsing around Suva, forgetting her imminent worries in the marine wonderland of the aquarium. Live sharks, turtles and coral-reef fish held her captive with their dangerous grace, antics and bright colours, until eventually she had to tear herself away, reminding herself that there was still plenty to see in the handicraft shops and pottery bazaars. She found an art gallery, too, which boasted some of the island's most beautiful landscapes, and, in one shop, actually bought a souvenir. A wood-carving of two identical figures, except that one was slightly darker than the other and seemed to merge with it like a shadow, Romy decided—or an insignificant twin. She didn't know why she bought it. She wasn't sure she even liked it, but it fascinated her for some reason.

She was still thinking about it as she came out of the shop, so deeply engrossed in her thoughts that she didn't look where she was going and was brought back sharply to her surroundings when she collided embarrassingly with someone.

'Tania!'

The man—flushed, tall and with a shock of unruly brown hair—was smiling down at her in recognition, and through her stammering apologies, Romy's heart sank. What had she let herself in for now?

'What's wrong? You look...as if you're seeing a stranger...'

How true that was! she thought wryly, her mind instantly forming the impression of a businessman under a lot of pressure from that creased, blue suit and that slightly harassed look, although he didn't appear to be any older than Aaron.

'I'm sorry,' she was saying quickly, forcing herself to continue her role as Tania. 'My mind was elsewhere, otherwise I'd have recognised you instantly.' Which was a blatant lie, she thought, cringing, stepping aside to let someone pass on the busy pavement. But she had to keep up the pretence somehow. For all she knew this man could well be a friend of Aaron's!

'You must have been preoccupied,' the man grimaced, making Romy wonder uneasily if she'd said the wrong thing—if this was someone else Tania knew well. But he didn't appear to be thinking anything was odd because he was asking, 'Look...how did you get here?'

When she told him that she had hired a taxi, he was insistent upon driving her home.

'That really isn't necessary,' Romy put in quickly, unaccustomed to accepting lifts from strange men. Neither did she relish the idea of having to pretend to be her sister for the whole duration of the journey home. But all her excuses, she realised disconcertedly, were being easily and swiftly quashed.

'I've got to virtually pass your door so it isn't any trouble,' he assured her, dispelling her last hope, and consequently she found herself seated in a low saloon, being driven through the countryside by a man she didn't even know!

A rather weak mouth sent a smile in her direction. 'So when did you get back?'

Trying not to remind herself how crazy this whole situation was, and to ignore the uncomfortable feeling that the man's eyes were rather too interested in her bare legs, Romy told him, and was rather relieved to find that he wasn't much of a conversationalist. He seemed content to make small talk for the whole journey, remarking how the sugar market was doing, and making the odd reference to his job—he was someone quite official in the Fijian Government by all accounts—and though Romy knew a few awkward moments when he started mentioning people she was supposed to know, she managed to wriggle out of giving straight answers with some very clever bluffing, coming to the conclusion that he was far less shrewd than Aaron Blake. Exactly who he was and how her sister knew *him*, she wasn't sure, but as he pulled up outside the house she became uncomfortably aware that his arm had slid across the back of her seat.

Mumbling a 'thank you' for the lift he'd given her, Romy made to get out, only to find that arm suddenly restraining her.

'What's the hurry?' she heard him query in a slightly offhand way. 'You didn't seem to mind too much last time... remember... at that party?'

Romy bit her lip, breaking out into a cold sweat. What party? she wondered numbly. God, what sort of mess had she got into now on Tania's behalf?

'If I recall,' he went on, his face too close to hers— the aftershave lotion he was wearing nauseatingly sweet, 'before you took off so unexpectedly last time, you did everything to indicate that you and I were going to be... well, you know...'

She knew all right! Inwardly, she flinched. So her twin was involved with this man, although Romy found it hard to believe. True, he was attractive in a rather obvious way, but he didn't seem her sister's type. And he made *her* skin creep!

'I've changed my mind since then,' she said quickly. 'I don't want any sort of involvement with anyone,' and hoped that would deter any further advances from him as she tried to get out of the car again. But she couldn't have been more mistaken.

She was being crushed painfully by arms that were neither tender nor considerate, and the mouth on hers was bruising in its quest for self-gratification. She tasted blood on the inside of her lip—heard the growl of another car as it passed, and forcibly—eyes blazing—she pushed him away, just in time to see Aaron's Ferrari take the bend on the hill with such aggression that its wheels were spinning in the dust.

'Next time you offer a lift to someone, make sure you tell them that it comes with conditions,' she spat, getting out and slamming the door.

And was surprised when he leaned out to call after her, 'You're not getting away with this! You led me on, and I'm coming around tomorrow night to get a few things straight with you!'

She didn't bother turning round as he pulled away, feeling near to exasperation. This situation was rapidly becoming a farce, she thought frustratedly, still unable to accept that Tania could have encouraged a man like that.

What on earth did she see in him? she wondered, shuddering, repelled by the memory of his mouth on hers. But her mind was more with the red car which was heading towards the big white house than with what had just happened with the man who had brought her home, because she had no worries about handling *him*. But Aaron must have thought she'd refused his invitation to lunch because she was seeing the other man and, judging by the way he had driven up that hill, he wasn't too pleased about it, either.

Well, let him be angry, she thought rebelliously, starting as a golden dove took off out of the trees near the front of the house. It was obvious he had no claim to her sister, otherwise Tania would have said *something*. When Tania became involved with anyone influential and attractive, Romy reflected with a wry smile, usually she made sure the world knew about her prize. And Aaron Blake would have been the greatest trophy of all!

She didn't like the turn her thoughts had taken as she went inside, and in a moment of inexplicable panic, sent up a silent prayer that Tania would contact her. She hated to admit this about Aaron, but she was afraid of him—of that ruthless streak behind that smooth, urbane veneer which she knew he would be quite capable of exercising if he thought he was being deceived, yet even more afraid of her own awareness of him whenever he came close, whenever he touched her. So why couldn't Tania pick up these waves of desperation, come to her rescue and ring her—tell her what to do? After all, they'd once been so close as to almost be able to tell what the other was thinking—feeling, practically. Wasn't that old telepathy between them still there?

If it was, it still hadn't shown itself the following day, and it didn't help matters at all to find that she still couldn't write anything that pleased her. It had been the same since her father had died, she thought, an intense ache of loss stabbing at her chest. She could never have realised how much she would miss his encouragement. He had been her moral support—her mental spur, she mused sadly and, in a moment's despair, wondered if she would ever write anything worthwhile again.

Deciding to take a break, she had the sudden urge to go for a swim, to ignore Aaron's order and wander down to the beach. But common sense stalled her. She had no wish to meet that reporter again, and it would be utterly foolish to risk being photographed by anyone while she was here. If pictures of her appeared in the newspapers as Tania, not only would she be guilty of an outrageous deception where a vast number of people were concerned, but things could become rather embarrassing if the deception were uncovered, she thought with a shudder. No, after everything that had happened up until now, she had no intention of moving far from this house until she could be Romy Morgan again. And so she sat down to write a short, conversational letter to Roger and was just beginning another to one of her old college friends, when the telephone rang.

CHAPTER THREE

'TANIA, dear!' a lively, feminine voice exclaimed.'Sandra Donnington here. Quintin Swain told me you were back.'

Romy's heart sank. She'd been hoping it *was* Tania and, with dismay, she realised how fast news of her sister's supposed return was spreading.

'I'm giving a party tomorrow night,' the voice continued down the line. 'Nothing dramatic...just eighty or so. You'll come, won't you?'

Stunned, Romy couldn't answer immediately, realising by the second that, when her sister had said no one here knew her that well, it simply wasn't true. She thought the world of Tania, but she did have this infuriating disregard for important facts—off the screen, anyway, Romy thought grimly. Like telling her Aaron was in Adelaide when in fact it had been Sydney, because that had been her twin's mistake, not hers.

'That's very nice of you, but...'

'No buts,' the woman interrupted as Romy tried to offer some excuse. 'I won't take "no" for an answer. And don't tell me you haven't got a thing to wear because I won't believe it! Cocktails are at eight-thirty and I shall be most offended if you don't turn up.'

Romy gulped, agitatedly coiling a strand of hair around her forefinger.

She couldn't go to a party! Mix with people who would think she was Tania! she thought, hectically. How would she know who to talk to? Who to smile at? What to say? She had to get out of going—that was definite. But how?

'I don't want to offend anyone...but I am rather busy tomorrow,' she prevaricated shakily. And, as a better excuse presented itself, quickly added, 'And I don't have any transport, anyway.'

Tania often hired a car here. Romy knew that. But there were times when she didn't, and as far as Sandra Donnington was concerned, this could well be one of those occasions.

'That's no problem. I'll arrange something. Eight-thirty it is, then.' And the line went dead.

Romy stood, still clutching the receiver, her mind in complete panic. She had never been reduced to such a state of hopeless agitation in her life. She didn't even know where the woman lived—where the party was being held!

Dropping the telephone on to its rest, she paced the floor, nibbling at a painted nail. It snapped and she cursed softly. Now that would mean getting out the nail repair kit, she thought exasperatedly, wishing she'd never agreed to this absurd pretence. How many people at this party would know Tania? she wondered, her stomach churning. And what would they expect her to talk about? Tania's world and hers were poles apart these days. And supposing she made some slip—said the wrong thing? However was she going to cope?

The thought mortified her and, feeling much too edgy now to carry on with her letters, she found her knitting and went out to sit on the veranda, trying to think of some way to get herself out of what she knew would be a disastrous evening—praying desperately for a brain-wave.

She was still there, engrossed in the purls and plains of a multi-coloured thing which didn't resemble any-thing wearable, when a sound made her turn.

Aaron Blake cut a dynamic figure against a back-ground of lush, tropical foliage, the khaki trousers and white, open-necked shirt he wore accentuating the grace and power of his limbs, and Romy's stomach fluttered nervously. With this continuing mental block, and the inevitable tense state she was in after all that had happened yesterday, and then that unsettling telephone call, *he* was all she needed!

His hair was brushed back—slightly damp, as if he had just showered, or swum, or both, she decided, as he came up the steps—a dark contrast where it curled over his snowy collar. The veranda boards creaked under his weight and, disconcertingly, his gaze came to rest on the soft outline of her breasts—braless and innocently tantalising beneath an Indian cotton top—and his lips pulled grimly.

'Are you expecting someone?'

Fortunately, the heavy shading along the high cheekbones masked the deepening colour which spread across them.

'Like whom?' she tried responding lightly, but it was difficult when she was doing her utmost to stuff her knitting down the side of her chair. It was disturbing enough just seeing him standing there, without being caught doing something very unTania-like into the bargain!

He didn't answer, his gaze falling to the horrendously bright wool she had been trying to hide, his profile strong and dark against the glittering blue of the sky.

'Expecting a cold spell?'

His mocking sarcasm assured her that all her efforts had been for nothing, and for a moment Romy froze. How would her sister have answered that?

Automatically, she laughed—made a careless gesture with her hand. 'Well . . . you never know!'

'In Fiji?' Aaron slipped his hands into his pockets, and the tanned forehead furrowed, amusement tugging at his mouth. 'At this time of the year?'

His curious glance made her lips compress and, too guilty to look at him, she dropped her gaze to the soft shirt—stretched tight across his chest—to that shadow of dark hair beneath—and a frisson of awareness shot through her. He was decidedly too virile. Too dangerously male, she thought, and wondered if Tania was as aware of that raw sexual magnetism as she was. She didn't see how any woman could be otherwise.

'There's something odd about you . . .'

His speculative words brought her head up to meet eyes which were studying her with such contemplative scrutiny that she could feel a cold sweat breaking out all over her skin.

So this is it! she thought, swallowing. The whole game's up!

But he was swinging away to look out across the garden—a tall, commanding figure who was no fool, she decided uneasily, getting to her feet. At least standing up she felt at less of a disadvantage.

'I've just been finding work hard-going lately,' she said, in an effort to quash his suspicions, following his gaze to the stark reds and creams of the bougainvillaea and gardenia growing side by side. Well, it was true, she mused. Even if he did think she was referring to television. 'I have to do *something* to unwind.'

He swung round, nostrils flaring above a grim mouth, saying with a quietly controlled anger, 'Like seeing Danny Gower?'

The man he had seen bringing her home yesterday? Was that his name? she thought, wondering, too, whether Aaron's obvious objection stemmed from jealousy. But that would mean that he had designs on Tania, she thought with a nervous shiver. In which case why hadn't he made it obvious yesterday? Had her twin rejected him at some stage? she wondered, incredulously. Was that why he was acting so coolly towards her now?

'So?' she taunted anyway, deciding that it wouldn't be a bad thing if he did think she was seeing the other man. It might make him stay away from her, so let him believe it if he wanted to.

A light breeze rustled the gardenias—an oddly disquieting sound—and seeing Aaron moving towards her, dark and predatory, Romy held herself rigid, more unnerved by him than she cared to admit.

'Is he this season's target?'

Clearly he disapproved of the frequency with which Tania changed her menfriends, not that Romy herself always understood her sister's sometimes fickle behaviour, but it was *her* business, and she almost told Aaron so. The icy look in his eyes, however, stopped her, and warily she pivoted away from him, moving inside.

'And what if he is?'

He chose not to answer as he followed her in, surprising her by completely changing the subject.

'I'm having people for dinner tonight...mainly business...but there's someone I feel you should meet. I thought you'd appreciate a few hours' warning.'

And that was an invitation?

Romy could feel her temper rising. For one thing, she didn't like the way he thought he could interfere in her sister's affairs, then dismiss the subject whenever he thought fit. And for another, she didn't like the way he seemed to think he could order her around. Well, he was going to be put straight about that!

'Just who do you think you are, coming down here and telling me what to do?' The shining gold bob swished wildly as she swung to face him, now with the protection of a safer distance between them. 'What business is it of yours whom I see here?' she challenged tartly. Or whom Tania sees? she added silently, wondering chillingly again what possible attraction this Danny could hold for her twin.

'None whatsoever.' Aaron's reply unbalanced her. Had she been wrong in assuming him to be jealous of the other man? she wondered frowningly, because his tone had been emotionless. The rugged planes of his face were inscrutable, only a muscle twitching in his jaw as he said with a dangerous softness, 'But perhaps you should try asking the same question of Danny's wife.'

His wife! She knew she must have looked shocked, but it was an effort to rearrange her features into more composed lines to avoid giving herself away. She could see now why Aaron was treating her twin with such contempt—why he'd made that cynical remark about marriage, too, on the beach yesterday, if Tania was carrying on with a married man. But she couldn't be! Romy refused to accept the idea, utterly shaken. Her twin had more scruples than that. Didn't she?

It took all her mental strength to remind herself that she was still supposed to be Tania, and somehow she met Aaron's eyes levelly, the cool blue of hers concealing her fear of him.

'Well, as you said... it's none of your business,' she uttered carelessly, turning away. And let out a small cry as he grabbed her wrist, spinning her round so fast that she almost lost her balance, only the strong arm which was pinioning hers behind her back keeping her vertical.

His gaze was flickering over her as if she were the lowest thing on earth, but there was an unmasked gleam of desire too, in those beautiful amber eyes, which called to a primeval need in her and brought warm colour creeping across her skin. His closeness electrified her. Even through her denim jeans she could feel the heat of his hips and thighs, and there were small beads of perspiration in the hollow of his throat where a pulse throbbed hard. That stirring, male scent of him was ravaging her senses, and despite her anger she was suddenly shocked to find herself craving the assault of that hard mouth—the violence of such a sick desire rocking her so much that, in the split second when he dipped his head, she panicked, twisting away from him with a muffled protest, and so forcibly that she collided with a small table, sending it toppling over.

Anger broken, she watched him stoop to upright the table—retrieve the wood-carving that had been sitting on top. He was studying the figurine with its shadowy counterpart pensively, a thin line between his brows. Holding her breath, Romy wondered what he was thinking. That it wasn't in the same taste as the other expensive ornaments about the place?

His gaze, cool and enigmatic, rested on her briefly, before he handed the carving back to her.

'I'll pick you up at eight,' was all he said decisively. And he left.

Still shaken from all that had transpired, Romy leaned against the door-jamb, massaging the tense muscles of her neck.

What on earth was she going to do? Aaron Blake was far too shrewd to continue playing this game with, and if she went to his house tonight she would be laying herself open to that razor-sharp perception. She wondered who it was he wanted her to meet, or rather Tania, she thought wryly. Going over to the hi-fi system, she put on a classi-cal record, hoping some soft music would relax her. It didn't, and a few minutes later she took it off again, considering how she could possibly get out of going tonight. If only she had listened to her better judgement and not been so stupid as to come here...

In desperation she rang the television studios again, in the vain hope that someone might have rung in and left a telephone number where the safari team could be contacted, but they hadn't, and Romy put the phone down, nibbling at her thumbnail.

Was Tania really playing around with a married man? The thought sickened her and she shied away from it, having always assumed Tania's ethics to be on the same level as her own. True, Tania was far more emancipated than she was, Romy thought, even though she herself could hardly be called innocent. She certainly wasn't a virgin. But one heartbreaking, teenage affair had taught her that she needed emotional commitment now before any physical relationship with a man, and even if her twin didn't share her view, she had always steered clear of other women's husbands. So why was she getting herself involved with one now? And Danny Gower had said he would be coming round tonight, Romy remembered, cringing. So if she didn't go to Aaron's, there would be that problem to contend with.

On the spur of the moment she considered ringing Aaron and telling him the truth. Ending this crazy pretence. The strain of having to watch everything she said and did. Wearing all this make-up! But if she told him now, not only would she show herself as the deceitful creature she was—render herself vulnerable to his raw anger when he realised he'd been made to look a fool— but blurting out the truth could well cost her twin this house, and she cared about her sister far too much to let that happen.

She would just have to go there tonight, she decided bravely, since the alternative was to stay here and suffer a visit from Danny Gower. And at least Aaron was single, she told herself, even if that sheer male magnetism of his did threaten her equilibrium. And after all, it wasn't as if she was going to be alone with him...

His house was as impressive inside as it was out. The hall floor was tiled in a kind of mosaic marble with an open staircase leading to the upper storey, exotic plants and foliage taking the eye to recesses and alcoves, the colour scheme tasteful in soft greens and beiges, the furnishings, Romy decided, expensive without being ostentatious.

Trying not to appear as though she hadn't been there before (she assumed Tania must have), she allowed Aaron to escort her into the main room. For a fleeting moment her mind registered a wall of well filled bookcases, original oil paintings, and, under her feet, the luxury of a thick, Indian carpet, but several pairs of eyes were looking interestedly at her, and beneath the creamy softness of a simple silk dress, she tensed.

Was she supposed to know any of these people?

Apparently, it seemed, she was, because the Alisons— a thin, middle-aged man with glasses and his dark-haired, rather effusive wife—greeted her like an old acquaintance. And when Aaron introduced her to a particularly distinguished, grey-haired man she frowned, wondering

where she'd heard his name before. Theo Stanley. It rang
a bell from somewhere. He even *looked* familiar.

'My cousin.' A smile played around Aaron's mouth
as he added, silkily, '*Your* landlord.'

Of course! The resemblance to Aaron was quite stag-
gering, she noticed now, wondering if it was nerves which
was making her so hot, or the humidity of the sultry,
tropical night. A bit of both, she reckoned, noting that
same high forehead—the proud, straight nose. He was
tall, too, as tall as Aaron, but much older and with a
curly, silver-grey moustache, though no less commanding for all that. In fact, between two such dom-
inant men it was difficult not to feel intimidated, she
decided when the preliminaries were over, especially when
she was going all out to deceive them!

Those familiar amber eyes were watching her—
weighing her reaction, she thought, uncomfortably. Then
she dismissed it as imagination. Tania had said she'd
never met her landlord personally, so her own surprise
could hardly have seemed out of place. Nevertheless,
she wished she hadn't come. Doing battle with Danny
Gower would have been preferable to this, she realised,
feeling sick.

'What will you have?'

Aaron's deep query shook her. What did Tania drink
these days? Agitatedly, Romy shifted her weight from
one foot to the other, aware that her host, looking particularly devastating in black trousers and a black silk
shirt, was waiting for her answer. She had to come up
with something—and fast!

She managed to pluck a spark of inspiration from the
air to murmur with a beguiling little smile, 'The usual?'

His hard gaze made her wonder if he noticed the
natural flush beneath the carefully applied make-up—
the way her pulses throbbed. But guilt was getting the
better of her again, she assured herself, when he responded almost immediately by bringing her a dry
martini.

The meal was superlative, she would have said, had she felt relaxed enough to enjoy it. Five courses consisting of the most well prepared seafood, meats, vegetables and fruit—during which she sat next to Theo Stanley who, she was grateful to admit to herself, did most of the talking. He was a widower, she discovered—living in New Zealand, and had spent most of his life in the property development business.

'But I've retired now and prefer to leave development to younger, thicker blood like my cousin's!' he told Romy laughingly. And then changed the subject completely by asking about her parents.

'My mother died when I was a child,' she explained to him. 'And my father . . .' She felt a lump in her throat and paused. 'Just three months ago.'

Across the table she noticed a flicker of something nearing sympathy in the depths of Aaron's eyes, though she hadn't even realised he'd been listening.

'I'm sorry,' he said, deeply. 'I didn't know.'

Because Tania hadn't been back here since then.

Emotion clouded Romy's eyes, and responding with a half-smile from glossy lips she looked away, reluctant that he should view her innermost feelings. Besides, Henry Morgan and her twin hadn't been that close, and Aaron could well know that.

She was relieved when he resumed talking to Richard Alison sitting next to him. An architect, Richard was here tonight, Romy had gathered, because Aaron wasn't totally happy with the man's plans for a small, industrial development—a project Aaron himself was financing. They were unsympathetic with the environment, she'd heard him say earlier, and changes would need to be made.

Almost unwillingly she found her attention held by the deep resonance of his voice, his control of the conversation and his surprising knowledge of the islands—her every sense too astutely aware of that dark, masculine presence. Then Theo was joining in with his contribution to the conversation, while Mona Alison was offering sweeping—and often, Romy thought, rather inane—statements of her own.

'What have you done to her tonight, Aaron...she's hardly spoken a word?'

Suddenly the talking had ceased and mortified, Romy realised that because of Mona's loud observation, everyone was looking at *her*. But what was she supposed to have said? she wondered, her throat going dry. She knew very little about Aaron's work here, other than what Tania had told her. That he was an environmentalist as well as a developer and that his new, yet unobtrusive developments had benefited the island considerably. Across the table she felt the inescapable pull of his gaze—saw him watching her the way a fox must watch a rabbit—and, pulse hammering, she gave a small laugh—strung with tension.

'With so many experts around the table I prefer to keep silent regarding things I know very little about.'

She shot a glance at Aaron and met the twist of something like amusement on his lips, though she couldn't think why.

'Yet you must have seen the changes in the time you've been coming here,' Theo's strong tones persisted to her utter dismay. 'Take the work that's going on in Lautoka for instance. Don't you think...'

'Excavations and drainage systems are hardly conducive to exhilarating conversation, Theo,' Aaron's deep voice came almost like a life-line to her rescue. 'I think most women would be utterly bored by them.'

'No, really...' she added quickly—truthfully—the smoky-blue shadow on her lids making her eyes appear a deep sapphire. 'I'm very interested...'

She noticed the line between Aaron's brows—the way he was studying her over the rim of his glass—and quickly she turned away, a throb of excitement surfacing with the sting of fear.

Could he know? Did that clever, hard-headed brain suspect the truth about her...that she wasn't the sophisticated girl he obviously usually entertained? Could he be playing with her? she wondered startlingly, considering the mockery in his eyes when she'd struggled to respond to Mona Alison's comment. Could he be testing her? Watching her squirm and relishing her discomfort until the moment she eventually cracked?

The wine, she decided, was making her over-imaginative, and she was more than relieved when Aaron suggested that they had coffee outside. The short walk to the terrace gave her chance to restore her equilibrium—dispel the wild flights of fancy she'd been nurturing inside.

Out here the night air was less stifling. A warm breeze came off the ocean, stirring the dark foliage of a small cypress tree near the steps. Way off, the lights of a moored yacht broke through the wall of darkness, casting beams on the restless waves. Romy breathed in deeply, catching the aroma of fresh coffee mingling with pine and the tang of salt air.

'I understand from Aaron that you're staying about a month this time.'

She tensed as Theo Stanley dropped down on to the seat next to hers and lit a cigar, the lighter's flame illuminating a profile that was as strong and indomitable as his cousin's. It was in the bloodline—that innate authority, a line of men who had been born to command.

'That's right,' she answered, keeping her eyes on the movements of a maid who was serving coffee, feeling her muscles tightening beneath the shoelace straps of her dress.

'Don't you consider it rather extravagant paying a year's rent on a house you use for just three months a year?' The authoritative mouth compressed, so much like the younger man's but with a hint of more compassion—less cynical, she decided, catching a strong waft of Havana, and knew whom she'd prefer to cross if it came to the crunch. 'Personally,' Theo expanded, in an uncompromising tone, 'I think it's a total waste of money.'

Romy sipped the hot beverage she had been given, taking her time. She had always thought it was a waste of money, too, how Tania insisted on keeping the house, although originally, Romy remembered, her sister had bought the lease for an extremely low price. And neither Theo nor his agents had been that strict about enforcing the three-months minimum-a-year clause—until now, when he wanted to sell. She guessed that he wouldn't think twice about withdrawing Tania's tenancy and going ahead with his plans if he found out that not only hadn't she come back to honour her contract, but that she had also sublet the place when the terms forbade it—even if it was to her twin! And what sort of trouble *she'd* be in if the deception was discovered, she dreaded to imagine!

Across the terrace, near the pool, she noticed Aaron standing, talking to the Alisons, and her throat constricted painfully. She would have to be careful.

'I agree...it must seem rather extravagant,' she responded smilingly, toying with the red necklace which enhanced the low neckline of her dress. 'But a job in television isn't all glamour. It can be pretty demanding,' she went on, explaining to him about the phenomenal pressures, the unsociable hours and how holidays away from it all were so essential. Which was quoting Tania perfectly, she thought, and with a wry smile at Theo, 'Life's tough at the top.'

The man sipped his own coffee thoughtfully, dropping his gaze to the long, red-tipped fingers of Romy's left hand.

'I'm surprised to see there's no fiancé or husband yet,' he commented, stroking his moustache, and absurdly, she felt her heartbeat quicken. 'If this was your permanent home you wouldn't be single for long. The men on these islands aren't as patient as those on the mainlands. The earth is fertile and yielding, and they like their women to be the same.'

Like true chauvinists, Romy bit back, her glance unconsciously going to Aaron, and she was startled to recognise a tug of desire. Shocked, too, to find that he was looking at her—his gaze unwavering and intense—and she flushed, turning away, for some reason embarrassed that he might have heard what had been said. Though how he had managed so far to escape the clutches of some woman with that immense, dark attraction, she couldn't altogether comprehend. He was the perfect male—intellectually as well as physically—and again she wondered why Tania hadn't said more about him. Was she immune to that hard, raw masculinity? she pondered incredulously. She couldn't believe that she could be. Even the middle-aged Mona was looking at him greedily, hanging on his every word, her laughter a little too loud, her response too obvious, making Romy cringe.

'Do you have any other family, Tania . . . brothers or sisters?'

Beside her, Theo was showing natural curiosity, but Romy's stomach churned. If they got on to that subject she could find herself telling one lie after another. And she sensed that Aaron was listening to them, too, now, even if he did seem politely interested in something the architect was saying, and that hard, dangerous perception behind the man was making her nervous and edgy.

'No one . . . except a sister,' she said quickly—slightly breathless—darting a glance around her for some means of escape.

'Older or younger?'

'What?' She met the elderly man's cool scrutiny with a tightening of her throat—a tense flutter of her eyelids. She had to get out of this situation—but how? She couldn't even excuse herself to go to the bathroom because she didn't know where it was! Nevertheless, she replied evenly, 'Older . . . but there's very little between us,' keeping to herself that the 'little' comprised minutes rather than years.

'Oh?' Theo clearly wanted to know more, and Romy swallowed, feeling Aaron's eyes on her again. She didn't know whether Tania had divulged to him that she had a twin. Probably not, if she had kept her promise, Romy guessed, otherwise he would have been sharp enough to work out the inconsistencies by now.

The thought made her shiver, despite the warm night. She had to end this conversation now. And as Mona's loud laugh distracted them, ringing out across the terrace, Romy grabbed her chance.

Mumbling some excuse about getting her jacket, she jumped up, only to feel the strap of her bag catch on the chair—tug out of her hand—and she gave a small cry of dismay as most of its contents scattered out over the ground.

Delayed, red with embarrassment, she scrambled to pick them up—lipstick, mirror, comb—the smile she gave Theo almost apologetic, though she tried not to look at Aaron as she made her hasty bid for the steps. And from behind her—bringing her up sharply—she heard his voice, deep and slightly mocking, say, 'Haven't you forgotten something?'

She turned quickly, following the direction of his gaze to the flat, black object peeping out from under her chair.

Her passport!

Colour washed up over her face, and she swung back, pulses quickening. God, how had she been so careless as to mislay that? Not only did it show a long-haired girl with glasses, but written proof of who she really was!

She made a clumsy effort to retrieve it, but Aaron got there first, and Romy held her breath as he stopped to pick it up, his long, tanned fingers closing around it.

'Thank you.' Somehow she managed to sound cool as she reached out to take it, then realised—unbelievingly—that he wasn't giving it back! Her heart came up into her mouth as he fingered the incriminating little document, the steadiness of his hands only emphasising just how hard her own heart was thumping.

'Most people look horrendous on these things,' he remarked, with a curl to his lips. 'What does a passport photograph do for a television glamour girl, I wonder?'

Sick with apprehension, Romy moistened her lips, her dress seeming to stick to her. If he opened it, that would be the end of everything. Tania's house. *Her* holiday—

for what it was worth! But worse, everyone here would
know how deceitful she was being, and that was the most
mortifying thought of all.

'Can I have it back...please?' She hadn't intended
to beg, but it was there—an element of supplication in
her voice—and he noticed it, evident from the way that
hard mouth quirked, that curious lift of his eyebrow. 'I
was in dire need of a hair-do that day!' she bluffed in
an attempt to make him comply, and with a little laugh,
'I look an absolute fright.'

'What do you think, Theo?' He was laughing softly,
his profile strong and unyielding, the long lashes black
against his tan. 'Shall we give it back to her?'

He could feel her fear—she was certain of it, caught
as she was in the dark hold of his gaze. She felt like
those moths which were beating their wings futilely
against the glass lanterns around the terrace—trapped
by a dangerous fascination. There was only she and he—
seemingly the others had ceased to exist—opponents in
a game where only one could win.

'Come on, Aaron...stop teasing her. Give it back.'

Theo's voice was threaded with puzzlement—as if he
were trying to make some sense of the tension which
sparked between the two of them. But, surprisingly,
Aaron was complying, his expression bored—like a cat
tired of playing with a mouse—and thanklessly Romy
snatched up the passport, relief seeming to sap her.

'Thank you,' she exhaled through gritted teeth, her
eyes two blue daggers of ice which would quite willingly
have stabbed him had they had the power to. And then
she was running down the steps, the derisive twist of his
lips imprinted on her mind as she sought refuge in a few
moments' privacy inside.

Did he know? she wondered, frantically opening un-
familiar doors in an attempt to find a cloakroom. Because if he did, then why hadn't he done something about
it? If he had any suspicions at all, she thought—miraculously finding a cloakroom through the third door she
tried—all he'd had to have done was to open that

passport and confirm them, expose her to his cousin, but he hadn't. So if he suspected *anything*, why had he let her go?

She shuddered, feeling again the intensity of that dark gaze—the latent sensuality behind it. Perhaps, as she'd thought earlier, he wanted to make her sweat, she considered angrily, brushing her hair with an unusual ferocity in front of the long mirror.

On the other hand . . .

Brush suspended, she studied her reflection. The soft, blonde bob, the heavily accentuated eyes and cheekbones, the darkly-creamed lips—could it be that he didn't really suspect anything at all? She looked unbelievably like Tania. Perhaps guilt was making her paranoid, she thought, self-mockingly, resuming her brushing, because wasn't it possible that he had simply been enjoying her discomfort out there, thinking that it sprang from vanity?

Gleaning confidence from that assumption, she made to go back to the terrace but, taking a wrong door, found herself in the main room again.

In the subdued light from a small lamp, the bookcases loomed invitingly. Keenly, she moved over to them, her gaze going along the shelves, curious to know more about the man—what sort of reading he preferred. There were the complete works of Shakespeare. Dozens of modern titles—both American and Australian—and a beautifully bound volume of the English writer, Thomas Hardy.

With tentative fingers she took it down from the shelf, blinking hard as she tried to read the small print inside. She'd had her contact lenses in too long and they were beginning to irritate her eyes. She felt like rubbing them, remembered the hours it had seemed to take to apply the shadow, eyeliner and applications of mascara, and stopped herself in time. It was hardly surprising her eyes were sore, she thought wryly. With all that, and the experimental attempts with shaders, blusher and lip-creams before she'd eventually achieved Tania's nocturnal look, her face felt like an artist's palette!

'Have some more light.'

She swung round, startled by the unexpectedness of the familiar, deep voice, her eyes adjusting as a centre-fitting suddenly illuminated the room.

'I—I came in for my jacket.' Damn! she was stammering, but she couldn't help it, feeling like a child caught doing something it shouldn't.

'Of course.' Aaron treated her to a half-smile, but he was closing the door and Romy stiffened, suddenly afraid. In black from head to foot he looked thoroughly intimidating, and alone with him she could feel all the confidence she'd summoned up in the cloakroom crumbling to dust.

'You know, you surprise me, Tania. I've never known you and Mona together without your managing to get into a heated argument with her, but I must congratulate you . . . you behaved impeccably tonight.'

Despite her better judgement, Romy couldn't check her anger, piqued firstly by the way he'd made her suffer out there, and now by his condescending tone.

'Really?' she retorted, hotly, knowing that Tania would probably have responded in exactly the same way to a man's superior attitude, only at that moment she wasn't trying to be her twin. 'And is there a prize for good behaviour, *sir*?'

Amused, his mouth was twitching at the corners, his voice softly suggestive as he said, 'Oh, yes.'

He was moving towards her, stalking across the Indian carpet like a dangerous, black panther. Romy swallowed hard, her heart hammering crazily.

Tell him you aren't Tania! a little voice shrieked inside of her. *Tell him now, before it's too late!*

But his threatening proximity held her rigid—tongue-tied—and she couldn't utter a sound.

CHAPTER FOUR

'THOMAS HARDY?' Aaron tilted the book Romy was still holding and a small tingle ran through her as his hand accidentally touched hers. 'Does he hold some appeal?'

She'd forgotten the book! Wildly, she almost blurted out that he was her favourite author, but stopped herself just in time. That would have been Romy Morgan speaking—not Tania—and anyway, her heart was beating so fast she could only respond unthinkingly with, 'Sometimes.'

Amber eyes widened, their depths cool and mysterious. 'For any particular reason?'

Romy shrugged, her hair a rich gold under the bright light.

'He's a good storyteller. What other reason is there?' she answered rather curtly, treading with extreme caution. How had they got on to this subject anyway?

A dark eyebrow lifted, the hard gaze examining—never leaving hers—so that nervously she touched her top lip with her tongue. He noted the gesture, the trace of a smile curving his mouth.

'He was a master of characterisation.'

Yes, he was, Romy thought, considering the Hardy volumes which had filled her father's study, every one of which she'd read again and again. But she couldn't share those experiences with Aaron Blake—didn't want to, even though she guessed that he could probably stimulate her intellectually with his own literary knowledge— so she said simply, her eyes guileless, 'Was he?'

The high forehead creased slightly. 'And very unpredictable.' Taking the volume from her, he snapped it shut, the movement causing a waft of his aftershave to drift tantalisingly towards her. 'He could fool anyone.'

His eyes were so probing that Romy's throat tightened. Now why had he said that? she wondered, apprehensively. Had she been wrong in assuming that he didn't suspect anything, after all?

She watched him place the book back in the empty hollow on the shelf, reaching it easily, though she had had to stand on tiptoe to do so, her eyes drawn to the play of muscles beneath the soft shirt.

'You never cease to surprise me, Tania.' He swung back to her with a curious half-smile. 'I wouldn't have thought your reading extended to much beyond your latest script...much less to the English classics.'

He was right, Romy thought, dismantled, tension coiling like a snake inside of her. Her sister seldom read, particularly fiction.

'There's probably a lot about me you don't know, Aaron Blake.'

Well, it was true, she thought wryly, lifting her chin to hide her fear of him. Then wished she hadn't because his gaze had fallen to the nervous little pulse beating in her throat—the perfect sweep of her shoulders, softly golden beneath the thin straps of her dress.

'Obviously.' His mouth tugged down at the corners and something lit the hard amber of his eyes—a fire so darkly sensual that Romy twisted away but was unable to escape the fingers which caught and tightened around her wrist. 'Like why you suddenly find the advances of a married man infinitely more preferable to mine.'

His words and his grip were cruel but she scarcely felt them, her mind registering with alarm the true meaning of what he'd said.

So Tania was on intimate terms with her landlord's cousin! But how intimate were they? Had they been lovers? she wondered riotously, her brain in such a whirl that it was difficult to think. Was Tania in love with him? The thought came to her startlingly. Although, if she was, why had she been seeing Danny Gower?

'I'd rather not talk about him,' she murmured as calmly as she could, trying to bluff her way out of what was now a dangerous situation, her pulse beating fast beneath the hard pressure of his thumb.

Did Tania's heart thump like this when he touched her? she wondered hazily. Because it wasn't just fear of him which was sending tingles along her spine.

'Well, I'm sorry, darling, because I want to,' he breathed, his tone threateningly cool, and Romy tensed, feeling the anger in him—the warmth of his body only inches from hers. 'Do you seriously think you can find any lasting happiness with another woman's husband?' he suggested abrasively, pulling her towards him so that she thought her heart would stop. That brooding sensuality was a dark threat, more, if anything, than his anger.

'Who said I'm looking for it?' she quavered, so weakened by that electrifying magnetism she was saying anything that came into her head.

'I see.' None too gently he lifted her chin with his fingers, tilting the heavily enhanced features to the hard, rugged planes of his. 'You're just looking for a good time. Well, that's fine by me, sweetheart, because I'm certainly experienced enough to give you that.'

Even if she'd known what was coming she couldn't have prevented it, because his arm was suddenly around her waist like an iron band and he was pulling her hard against him, his strength making a mockery of her efforts to resist him as he took her mouth with his own.

She'd never been kissed like this in her life. Shock-waves of desire flooded through her—sensational and frightening, an intensity of hunger so great that she gave herself up totally to the unyielding demands of his mouth. She felt his hand move to the small of her back, pressing her against the rock-hard solidity of his body, and she made a small sound in her throat, a pleasurable anguish stabbing at her loins.

Oh God, she wanted him! So much so that when his hand slid up to cup her breast she arched instinctively towards him, her body craving the pleasure he alone could give her.

Her heart thundered beneath his. She felt as if she were drowning and clutched at him so that she wouldn't sink, exciting little tingles running through her as she felt the sinews tauten with desire beneath the fine shirt.

'Tania . . .'

She stiffened, fighting the persuasion of his lips against her throat—the almost hypnotic scent of him—to push away from him in sudden shame.

'No!' she protested shakily, logic and reasoning surfacing so sharply it was almost a pain.

'Why not?' His eyes were slumbrous—darkened by desire—though his mouth was held in a firm line of control. 'Your body still wants me . . . as much as it ever did if that response was anything to go by . . . so why don't we carry on as before . . . beginning tonight?'

'No, I . . .' What could she say?

Breathlessly, she tried to assimilate her thoughts, her hands against his chest trying to hold him at bay, her long, scarlet nails a vivid contrast against the startling black.

So there was no doubt about it, she realised in a daze. He and Tania were lovers! And now he thought that she, Romy, would . . .

In a moment of blind panic she almost blurted out the truth. Then stopped herself when she thought of how unashamedly she had responded to his kiss—the intimate caress of his hands. How could she explain that? She couldn't—even to herself. So what would Aaron think of her? That her morals were obviously as questionable as he thought Tania's were?

'I've got a headache,' she prevaricated instead, and cringed from the absolute triteness of her excuse.

He didn't believe her. That was obvious from the sceptical twist of his lips. But he said simply, his hand cupping her chin as he looked down into her flushed face, 'Well, we have a whole month, don't we?' which sent a tingle of apprehension along her nerve-endings and put her on edge for the rest of the evening, though he didn't refer to it or try to touch her again, even when he drove her home.

The next morning she woke with a raging headache. Which will just teach me not to tell lies, she thought with a painful grimace as she tried to wash away the cobwebs of a disturbed night under the cool spray of the shower.

She'd spent hours last night, tossing and turning, her mind buzzing with endless questions. Like, how long had her sister and Aaron been lovers? How much did he mean to Tania? And why, when she could have such a supreme specimen of masculinity as that, had she chosen to transfer her interest to a man like Danny Gower? She had always looked up to her twin—admired her—but now, uneasily, Romy found herself questioning her sister's life-style—her relationships with men. Had what she'd always assumed to be occasional, harmless self-indulgence on the part of her fun-loving twin been, or become, out-and-out promiscuity? She hated herself for thinking it about the sister she'd grown up with—loved deeply—but what other explanation was there for Tania's behaviour? she wondered unhappily.

And last night Aaron had seemed determined to reclaim what had obviously been his.

She had to get away—today! Just the thought of the previous evening threw her into a panic. She couldn't—wouldn't!—go along with this deception any longer. And even if she could—which her common sense wouldn't even let her consider—then she would only be putting her own emotions on the line, because she was more strongly attracted to Aaron Blake than she'd ever been to any man. And with an intensity which frightened her.

Stepping out of the shower and towelling herself dry, she pulled on white, cotton slacks and a red, V-necked top, studying her figure in the mirror.

It was a perfect duplicate of Tania's. Small, firm breasts. Gently curving hips and long, slender legs. Only it lacked one thing—the sexual sophistication. Why else would she have felt so out of her depth when Aaron had kissed her? she thought, with a sensual shudder. But she knew why. Because one brief affair hadn't exactly schooled her for a man like that. It had been to a boy at college that she'd given her heart and then her body so generously, ensnared as she'd been by the idle promises of first love, when she'd been too naïve to realise that it wasn't mutual and couldn't last. And, of course, it hadn't, she remembered wryly—starting to blow-dry the soft, blonde hair—and she'd found out soon enough when he's transferred his affections to another girl. But that first bitter experience had made her wary of relationships, other than the easy, uncomplicated camaraderie she shared with Roger. And often, the other men she dated seemed to want to use her as a stepping-stone to Tania, she reflected—her gaze absently going to the little double figurine which now stood on the dressing-table—so that sometimes she felt as if she'd lost her own identity in the wake of her twin's success.

Anyway, she'd hardly had the sort of grounding to be able to handle a man like Aaron, and the disturbing prospect of further intimacies with him motivated her into making a decision.

Fighting back the nagging feeling that she was letting her sister down badly, she rang the airport, only to be told that there wasn't a vacant seat on any flight out that day. Exasperated, Romy booked one for the following day and, keen to make some progress towards leaving, started packing, hoping desperately that Tania would understand.

'Well, if she doesn't, she's some sister,' she muttered, half angrily, wondering how her twin could have let her walk into such a complicated mess. Coming here had brought her nothing but one embarrassment after another. Like Danny Gower for a start, who *had* called last night according to Niki, and then taken off in a huff when he'd heard she was with Aaron. And this party tonight, which with all that had transpired, she'd almost forgotten about. She shuddered, realising that each hour that passed brought it closer and she still hadn't worked out how she was going to get out of attending. Perhaps she could have a migraine, she thought suddenly, which would see her very nicely through until tomorrow. And if taking off like this did cost Tania this house, well, didn't she herself have just as much to lose by staying here?

There was her self-respect for a start, which was sadly fraying round the edges as a direct result of this deceit. And her morals, threatened by a small, primeval need inside of her which, after last night, warned her that if she was foolish enough to stay here for any length of time, she could well end up craving the advances of her sister's lover...

The thought shamed her into realising how little resistance she had against him and, on edge, afraid that he might call, she closed her suitcase and decided to go for a long walk, trying to shrug off the memory of his kiss, the way she'd so wantonly invited his caresses.

Last night, she thought, trudging down a narrow, overgrown path, she had used his invitation purely as an escape from one awkward situation, only to find herself in a far worse one!

A bright turquoise bird shot out of the sighing green fronds of a treefern, and absently she watched as it soared away into the blue. In the distance, the ocean sang its eternal song, the white-crested waves sparkling in the sunlight—beckoning her.

She craved a swim. Her hand shielding her eyes, enviously she watched a speedboat some way off pulling a skier across the blue surface, and it took all her willpower to stop herself going down to the beach. She didn't want to risk meeting *anyone*, she told herself, but knew deep down that it was Aaron whom she was so anxious to avoid. And not so much because of her fear of him, she found herself unwillingly admitting, as of the fear of her own feelings—the unbidden, physical responses he could evoke in her.

All at once she realised that she had lost the path. The trees were growing more abundantly around her, and she wasn't sure which way she had come. She had been walking for at least half an hour, she realised, glancing at her watch, and though she couldn't see the sea any more she could still hear it, louder now, if anything. With only that to guide her, she pushed on through the trees, her ears attuned to the hum of insects and the pure, clear song of some tropical bird way off to the left. But it was another half-hour before she emerged from the jungle of dense foliage—hot and dishevelled—and found herself on a lonely, rough road. Although there *were* tyre marks in the dust, she noticed gratefully, deciding that if she followed them they might lead to the village where Niki lived, or even back to the house.

What she wouldn't give for a cool shower!

Even as she thought it, she heard the purr of a car engine in the distance and half considered flagging it down to ask the way. But as she turned and saw the car come into view, her heart missed a beat and then sank. The Ferrari was already slowing down.

'Would you care for a lift?' Aaron's eyes mocked as they took in the dishevelled blonde hair and flushed cheeks, and it was obvious that he knew she was lost. Which was why he was looking so amused, she thought, irritated, and on impulse wanted to refuse. But she would probably have to walk miles if she did, she realised frustratedly, and martyrdom never had been her scene. So there was only one thing to do.

'I wanted a walk,' she said, nonchalantly, wishing she could wipe the smug look off his face as she slid on to the warm leather beside him. 'I didn't realise how far I'd gone.'

His eyes flashed a hard glance at her as he set the car into motion.

'You must have a lot on your mind.'

Romy pressed her lips together, refusing to be provoked or intimidated by his somewhat caustic remark. He probably thought she'd been lost in her desire for Danny Gower!

She cast a glance over his silver-grey business suit immaculately teamed with a white shirt and silver-grey tie, her stomach doing funny things.

'And I suppose you just happened to be passing?' she rejoined tartly, desperately regretting that she hadn't been able to get a flight out that day. What she should have done was to have taken her cases and booked into a hotel this morning to avoid seeing him again, she realised, reproaching herself for not doing so. But it was too late now to consider what she *should* have done.

'Actually, I *was* looking for you,' he told her, changing gear.

She gave him a cautious look, her eyes guarded. 'Oh?'

'Sandra Donnington mentioned that she's asked you to her party. I came down to offer you a lift.'

He was going! For one wild moment she knew a swift comfort in the thought, because she hadn't altogether convinced herself that the migraine excuse would sound plausible, particularly as she'd shown some reluctance to attend initially. And if she had to go, absurd though it was, suddenly she was desperate for this man's support. After all, he was the only person on the island she felt she knew and with him beside her tonight, at least she'd have a crutch to lean on, she thought rashly, until she made herself see sense. To attend that party alone would be utterly foolish. To attend with *him* would be positively suicidal—where her equilibrium was concerned, anyway! So she said, curtly, turning away, 'No, thank you.'

She felt his eyes on her—cool and reflective. 'Saving your attentions for Danny Gower?' The car growled menacingly as Aaron changed down to take a bend. 'I'm sure he'd have bent over backwards to take you if he knew, my dearest . . . but I understand he's escorting his wife.'

Romy shot a glance across the space between them, glimpsing his strong profile from beneath lowered lashes. There was a glitter of contempt in his eyes, a set to the hard jaw and firm, unrelenting mouth which assured her in no uncertain terms what he thought about her. Tania had certainly lost this man's respect, even if he still wanted her, Romy cogitated uneasily, wishing she didn't have to be the one to feel the lash of his tongue. But she had set out to deceive—however indirectly in the beginning—and now she supposed she was only having to pay for that foolish misdemeanour—and it probably served her right!

'I'm not going,' she responded quietly, shuddering from the thought of what she could be letting herself in for if she did. Because she'd just decided that as soon as Aaron dropped her off, she was going to finish her packing and ring for a cab as she should have done hours ago, and find a hotel in Suva.

'We'll see about that.'

The determination in him made her look at him hard, but he didn't take his eyes off the road, and Romy turned away with a rebellious set to her lips. So he thought he could make her go. Well, was he in for a surprise!

Waving grasses of bamboo caught her attention on her side of the car, and other golden grasses she couldn't name stretching away to the very edge of a pine forest— timber the Fijians grew for commercial use, she remembered absently, anxiety about Tania gnawing at her.

Why, she asked herself worriedly, would a girl who could have any man she wanted get herself involved with another woman's husband? It wasn't like Tania to do a thing like that. And what had happened between her and Aaron to make her want someone else? she wondered puzzlingly, because she couldn't help thinking, with a small tremor of excitement, that a man like him could probably satisfy the most discerning female.

'Where are we going?'

Surprisingly, they had reached Tania's house, but Aaron wasn't stopping. Instead, he was swinging the powerful car up the hill.

'Swimming,' he said, laconically.

Romy frowned. 'Swimming?'

Aaron's eyes remained on the road. 'You're in need of some instruction, remember?'

She felt the web of her own deceit tightening insidiously around her.

'I can't.' She said it too quickly, a hint of panic in her voice. She couldn't stand this another minute. She couldn't! The deceit. The strain of trying to outwit him. And then there was that dangerous magnetism of his that she wasn't sure how to cope with...

'I don't have a swimsuit,' she reinforced, a little more steadily.

The hard mouth twitched. 'Since when did that ever bother you?'

'What?' She looked at him aghast. It might not bother Tania, but if he thought *she* was going skinny-dipping with him, he had another think coming!

'Why the false modesty?' He sent her an enquiring look. 'It's never worried you before. And if you're concerned about Theo, don't be,' he advised silkily. 'He's spending the day with friends. And Raku's gone out with Niki, so we'll be quite alone.'

Quite alone! Beneath the cool, red top Romy could feel herself breaking out into a sweat. This can't be happening to me! she thought, mortified, twisting red-tipped fingers agitatedly through her hair. Heaven knew! she was no prude. But swimming naked with a man she barely knew—and one as devastating as Aaron Blake— *that* was definitely out of the question!

'Won't you find it rather distracting?' she suggested, colour stealing across her skin, so disconcerted she was in complete danger of giving herself away. 'I mean...if you're going to teach me to swim...'

'Don't worry,' he smiled lazily, pulling up outside the big house. 'I think I might just be able to control my urges until the lesson's over.'

Oh, God! This had gone too far. As he came round to open her door, she searched wildly for some excuse to get herself out of this awkward situation. And decided that the only possible way now was to tell him the

truth. After all, if he cared enough about her twin, would
he in fact be likely to say anything to Theo that would
jeopardise her tenancy—and his own chances of seeing
her again?

'Aaron...' she started shakily, getting out of the car,
her lids trembling as her eyes refused to meet his strong,
dark features. And then the sound of a window opening
made them both look up, and beside her she heard him
curse softly.

'Well, aren't you just disappointed!' she taunted
lightly, her tension releasing itself on a tight little laugh
at the sight of Raku mending a broken window.

But was that disappointment she read in his eyes?
Baffled, she thought it looked more like the hard gleam
of victory than anything else.

As he led her inside, anxiously she wondered if he
thought there was anything odd about her modesty in
the car. And then decided that he probably assumed she
was reluctant to share past intimacies with him because
she was interested in someone else. Anyway, what did it
matter since she was leaving in a few hours?

'You left a bikini here on one occasion last time, remember?' he pointed out to her, making her realise, with
dismay, that she still wasn't going to be able to wriggle
out of this swimming lesson. And, with a toss of his
chin, 'You'll probably find it in one of the drawers in
the main guest room. I'll be out as soon as I can.'

With no indication of where the main guest room was,
naturally!

By day, the house looked more vast than ever, and
uncertainly Romy ascended the stairs, aware of Aaron's
dark gaze following her as he started making a telephone call from the hall below. He was still working,
she realised, reaching the top of the stairs, and glancing
back, saw that he was still watching her, his thoughts
concealed by the cool mask of his features.

She gave him a dubious smile, and bit her lower lip.
God! Did she go left or right? She felt the hairs rising
on the back of her neck. Tania would *know*!

She shot a furtive glance back at Aaron, who, to her relief, had turned away, totally engrossed in conversation with someone. Then she plumped for the latter, her heart sinking when she saw the numerous doors which flanked the carpeted corridor, and the portly Raku just coming out of a room at the end of it.

Which was the main guest room? Desperately she scanned the line of highly glossed white doors. Raku would think it very odd if she opened the wrong one by mistake.

But her worries were unfounded, because as she approached he opened the door nearest him. His manners were as superlative as his employer's, she noted absently, and tried not to sound too relieved as she thanked him.

She found the bikini almost at once in a chest of drawers—a minuscule piece of nothing Tania sometimes obviously considered too much, and heat prickled across Romy's skin as she remembered what Aaron had expected of her.

Thank goodness for Raku! she reflected, changing. He'd unwittingly helped her out of two embarrassing situations within the space of about five minutes!

Coming outside, she found that the air was humid and still. Sunlight shone on the pool, making it sparkle a vivid turquoise, the creamy gardenias which fringed it exuding a fragrance which was heady and evocative. There was no one about and she had the almost irresistible urge to plunge in—lose herself in the clear, blue depths—but a strong effort of will restrained her. She wasn't supposed to be able to swim, was she?

'Very nice.'

She turned sharply. Aaron was watching her, his eyes resting appreciatively on the tenuous lines of her body, and she blushed, wishing she'd been able to bring one of her own, less revealing swimsuits. This one was no more than two wisps of scarlet, secured by the flimsiest of strings!

'Are you ready?'

He had changed, too, the immaculate business suit substituted for a pair of dark bathing trunks which revealed most of that magnificent male torso, and Romy gulped.

I'll never be ready, she thought, too aware of him to feel comfortable. And trying to delay the inevitable, murmured, almost in an appeal to him, 'It's so hot. Couldn't I just paddle?'

'No.'

His tone dispelled argument and she watched as he moved to dive off the side of the pool, his body arched, displaying the grace and power of a wild animal as it broke the surface of the water, the perfect movements of his long, lean physique fascinating her, bringing goosebumps to her arms. He surfaced, shaking water out of his eyes with a swift toss of his head.

'Come on . . . in!'

Gingerly—pulse hammering—she obeyed, using the steps like a beginner, and as she reached the last one she felt Aaron's hands go around her waist—lifting her down—and she caught her breath sharply, electrified by his touch. He probably thought her reaction was from the shock of the water. She certainly hoped so!

'Nervous?'

There was a twist to the sensuous mouth—a curious glitter in the amber eyes, and she answered without a shred of dishonesty, 'As hell!'

She didn't know how she got through the next forty-five minutes. Aaron seemed intent on putting her through every basic stroke imaginable, which didn't help to ease her conscience at all. But she put up a good performance of pretending to be unable to swim, even managing once to simulate a futile grab for the side, with a subsequent and convincing show of panic, unaware of how close Aaron was. Finding herself caught embarrassingly in her instructor's arms, she then wished she hadn't been so stupid.

'I'm all right.' She was as choked as if she'd really been in danger of drowning, but it was the feel of that broad, bronzed chest beneath her hands that was robbing her of breath. Sliding her fingers over the drenched cap of her hair, she tossed away the rivulets which were streaming down her face, and opened her eyes to a gaze that was scrutinising yet inscrutable.

'You'd have made it if you hadn't lost concentration at the last minute and brought your head up,' he said tonelessly, and she felt an intense pang of guilt. If only he knew!

Then he was releasing her, and in spite of everything she felt the cold loss of his arms. But she couldn't relax with him at all after that and, though contact with him was casual, she found herself fighting a strong and startling reaction every time he touched her.

Eventually she couldn't stand it any longer and pulled away to grab the tiled edge.

'You're a taskmaster,' she pretended to accuse, breathless not from any physical exertion, but from the shocking realisation that she *wanted* this man to touch her.

He smirked, his own hair glistening with droplets of water from her unceremonious splashing earlier.

'When I give lessons in *anything*, Tania, I like to make sure they won't be forgotten.'

There was a hard gleam in his eyes and Romy shuddered. She could believe that! If he found out I wasn't Tania after all this effort, he'd probably drown me, she thought, gulping, apprehension motivating her into clambering out.

She didn't make it. A strong hand was closing around her slim ankle, and with a small, startled cry she was being pulled back into the water, her body suddenly rife with sensation as it came up hard against the unyielding strength of Aaron's.

'What are you doing?' Her voice was strung with panic—every muscle in her body tensing as his arms locked around her.

'Call it accepting payment for services rendered.'

No! her mind rebelled—trying to push him away. He was Tania's lover, not hers!

But his mouth on hers was a hungry demand—his kiss blotting out all else. The hard, wet leanness of his body burned against her own nakedness, the alien and alarming sensations which sprang to life in her denying her the strength to refuse him. Her head tipping back, she clutched at him, feeling the broad sweep of his shoulders like damp velvet beneath her hands, and she heard his breath catch—thought he gave a low groan as his lips left hers for the inviting satin of her throat.

Around them the water lapped sensuously—adding kindling fuel to her arousal—and she was trailing her fingers slowly down his back, delighting in her own feminine power as she felt the muscles tighten—heard his deep groan of appreciation.

She was being lifted off her feet, those strong hands against her hips raising her up so that his lips could trail a fiery path to the valley between her breasts. And then his lips closed over one, the warmth of his mouth burning through the flimsy scarlet of her bikini top, the intimacy making her gasp with such an earth-shaking explosion of desire that she shuddered.

She heard an insect hum—somewhere in another world, it seemed, the only reality Aaron's lips and hands and what they were doing to her.

She could feel the evidence of his own arousal against her, his breathing heavy and ragged, and then his teeth were tugging at the impeding silk which covered her breast, drawing it aside to taste the soft, pure honey of her femininity.

'Aaron...'

She didn't even know she had spoken his name—lost on a tide of warmth and pleasure and sensation as his tongue teased the rosy, taut peak of her breast, sending a surge of spiralling need through her loins.

He caught her to him, burying his lips against the sensitive column of her throat, and his voice was husky—thick with desire.

'Oh, God, you're beautiful.'

And then she stiffened, shamed by her wild, abandoned response. Of course, he was making love to Tania...

She didn't know how it had been possible to forget that, but she remembered it now, coldly and shamefully, and hurt pride stung her with an intense and burning degradation. And then Aaron lifted his head, his breathing ragged, the dark features flushed with passion, and guilt-ily Romy realised just how near he was to being out of control. Her own breathing was fast and shallow, trapped as she still was in the demoralising clutches of her desire. Dimly, she heard a shrill sound which seemed to be coming from a long way off, but she couldn't assimilate what it was. Instead, she was wondering why Aaron was looking at her as if he hated her. And then she remembered. Tania was seeing another man, so he probably despised himself for the way he thought she could still make him feel.

'Don't you think one of us had better answer the phone?' His words were cutting and cold.

So that was what it was.

Numbly, Romy watched him swim away from her and at the other side, haul himself effortlessly out of the water, and quickly she straightened her bikini top, burning with shame.

Why had she let him go that far? Did she have so few principles that she could seduce her sister's lover without turning a hair? she wondered, getting out of the pool. And under the pretence of being Tania? If he ever found out...

A cold tingle ran the whole length of her spine. She would never be able to face him again, she thought, colour scorching her cheeks, only relieved that after today she wouldn't have to.

'I've got to go out,' he said, coming back to where she was sitting on one of the loungers—towelling her hair; and she looked up at him, surprised. In the short time he had been inside he had changed back into his suit again, and Romy lowered her gaze, finding this devastating executive image grossly unsettling after their too-recent ardour in the pool.

'When you're ready, Raku will drive you home,' he stated coldly, staring down at the perfect structure of her face—the sweep of colour on the high cheekbones not escaping that inscrutable regard. 'I'll be down to pick you up later for Sandra's party.'

She looked up at him then, but he was striding away, obviously not intending to stay and argue with her.

What was the point, anyway, of reiterating that she wouldn't be going? she thought, sliding off the lounger. Let him realise it for himself when he'd discovered that she'd gone.

A few moments later she heard the car engine start up, then the Ferrari growl away, and a few moments after that, all was quiet.

She wouldn't see him again. It suddenly struck home hard, and she felt a swift, sharp stab under her rib-cage. Angrily, she reached for the blue wrap which Aaron had brought out for her, annoyed that it should matter so much. Good heavens! she'd only known the man three days, so why was she letting him affect her to this degree? It was Tania he wanted, she reminded herself sharply, and even if it wasn't, she didn't think *she'd* relish coping with such a dominating character. Oh, he could probably make her feel incredible in bed, she thought, fastening the belt of her wrap and trying to ignore an unwelcome tug of desire in her loins. But out of bed they would probably be at each other's throats, because he was far too sure of himself, and she wasn't the type to be bossed around by any man.

The pool was still and blue—deliciously tempting—and Romy hesitated before going inside.

Goodness, she needed a swim! A real work-out to ease these tensions which had built up in her over the past few days—the frustration and shame she was suffering from her uninhibited response to Aaron's lovemaking—to cleanse the feel of him from her skin.

Raku was doing some work in the garage—she'd heard him telling his employer earlier—so there was no one around to see...

Ripping off the towelling wrap, she was running back on tiptoe to the tiled edge as if her feet had wings. Poised, she took a deep breath and was suddenly springing— plunging down into the millpond stillness of the pool.

The first dive was invigorating, taking her breath away, but within seconds she had recovered, cutting through the blue wall of water with an athlete's grace, twisting and diving as wildly as a fish imprisoned in a keep-net too long and then suddenly released. She plunged down again into the silent, blue depths, touching the bottom before pushing up to glide with long, lithe strokes just below the surface for the whole length of the pool. Turning; somersaulting into another dive; staying underwater until she reached the other end where she surfaced, grasping at the tiled edge.

Tossing her wet hair out of her eyes, she gave a small sob of satisfaction, the sound instantly turning to one of horror when she saw the feet planted determinedly apart, only inches from her fingers, her gaze riveted on the immaculate grey shoes.

CHAPTER FIVE

'WELL, well...the lady can swim. And so well she could teach *me* a thing or two!'

Impaled, Romy couldn't utter a word, the anger in Aaron's eyes so intense she couldn't even think. And as she tried to ease herself up out of the water, he reached down and caught her arm, hauling her effortlessly to her feet. She swayed unsteadily against him, wincing from the pain of his grip, and absently noticed the dark patches which were forming on his suit from her wet body, the splashes on his shoes.

'Surprised to see me?' His tone was caustic, his eyes narrow slits in the hard structure of his face as Romy tried to offer some lame excuse for lying to him. 'Well, I'm going to get some explanations out of you,' he interrupted harshly, drowning her attempts to try and bluff her way out of trouble. 'And you're going to give them to me *now*, Romy Morgan!'

He knew her *name*? She darted a look at him, her eyes frightened. 'How—how did you find out?' she stammered, tremulously.

Roughly, he twisted her round so that she fell back on to the sun-lounger with something of a thud, and stood looking down at her with his thick, black brows drawn together.

'I think I'm the one entitled to the answers.' His expression was stern—his voice quietly controlled. 'What sort of bloody fool did you think I was?'

Water trickled down from her hair on to her shoulders and, despite the tropical sun, Romy shivered, recoiling from his anger and feeling rather self-conscious in her scanty bikini while Aaron was so formally dressed.

'I've never thought you were a fool,' she sniffed, the water making her nose run. And, determined not to be intimidated, added rebelliously, 'And don't swear at me.'

Aaron's mouth pulled down grimly. 'Why not? Tania can give as good as anything she gets when the mood takes her... and you want to be Tania, don't you?' He dropped down on to his haunches so that his eyes were level with hers, two amber spheres of anger meeting the wary mutiny of cornflower-blue.

'I didn't think I'd be deceiving anyone,' she began, thinking how ridiculous that sounded. 'You were supposed to be away and...'

'And it came as quite a blow to your mutual little plans to find out that I wasn't.'

Romy swallowed, trying not to notice how tight the grey trousers were stretched over his thighs—how the broad chest lifted heavily beneath the snowy-white shirt. The sun was picking out the highlights in his hair—red as fire against the bitter chocolate—and she turned away, sniffing again, looking hopelessly for her bag. But she had left it inside, and she was surprised when Aaron tossed a clean, white handkerchief into her lap. It bore that pleasant, manly scent of him, she noticed, when she picked it up.

'It was only so that Tania wouldn't lose the house,' she admitted, blowing her nose and deciding that there was room only for the truth now. In a way it was a relief to be telling him. 'Tania couldn't make it... and I... I thought it would be a marvellous idea to come here and try to finish my book,' she went on, wanting to attach most of the blame to herself. After all, he couldn't know how much she'd objected to Tania's idea initially. And this way he might be more understanding towards her twin, even if he looked angry enough to kill them both at this precise moment. 'I write,' she confessed, rather shyly.

'I know.' Aaron gave an irritated grunt and got to his feet, stuffing his hands deep into his trouser pockets. And when she looked at him questioningly, he said, 'I

checked up on you. The flight offices were very co-
operative. After that...a few telephone calls to Melbourne put me very nicely in the picture. I knew Tania
had a sister, but I hadn't realised until yesterday that
you were identical twins. Then...all the loose pieces
slotted into place.' He grimaced, a muscle moving in his
jaw. 'So I thought I'd string along with you for a
while...play a little game of my own. I knew it wouldn't
be too long before you made some obvious slip.'

Romy stared at him, her eyes wide, disbelieving. The
swimming lesson. Those mortifying moments with the
passport. And those intimate kisses. He must have
known then...

'You...' Unspeakable adjectives flew to her lips, but
she stemmed them in time. After all, she'd been no less
unscrupulous than he had. Absently, she watched a
brightly coloured butterfly settle on the creamy blossom
of a gardenia, its delicate wings trembling in the warm
air.

'How...how long have you known exactly?' she asked
quietly.

The broad shoulders shrugged beneath the expensive
jacket. 'Let's just say I *suspected* something all along.
Something wasn't right with you. The knitting. Com-
ments you made which didn't quite tie up. And there
were other things...'

He turned to stare out across the sparkling pool, his
hands still in his pockets, and then he swung back, the
strong angles of his face condemning as he looked down
at her.

'Just how far were you prepared to go?'

Romy tensed, moistening her lips, and hot colour crept
into her cheeks. She'd been dreading that he'd get around
to that.

'What do you mean?' she asked uncertainly, playing
for time.

'I mean...would you have jumped into your sister's
bed as well...accommodated her lovers?' he enquired

of her scathingly. 'Was that all part of the service in the
name of sisterly love?'

'No!' She threw the word at him, shame chastening
her, and felt his condemnation burning against her like
tangible fire. 'Of course I wouldn't have...' She broke
off, her mouth twisting with disgust that he should even
think so, still not fully able to accept that the twin she
loved—respected—was so casually sleeping around.

She flinched as he reminded her, sneeringly, 'No? Then
what about those not-so-innocent kisses we exchanged?
After dinner last night.' And as she opened her mouth
to speak, 'Oh yes...that's right.' This was punctuated
by a humourless laugh. 'You feigned a headache, didn't
you? But what about this morning? Not half an hour
ago?' He moved closer to her, causing her pulses to
throb—her breasts rise and fall sharply beneath the
fragile silk of the bikini top. 'Were you planning to call
a halt at some stage? Because if you were, you were certainly leaving it a bit late! Or would you have let me...'

'No!' She jumped up, pressing her hands over her nose
and mouth, still clutching his handkerchief. She'd never
felt so ashamed in her life. All she knew was that she
had wanted him physically as she had never wanted any
man, and she didn't know how she would have reacted
if he hadn't reminded her that he was making love to
Tania...

She looked at him, her blue eyes glittering angrily.
'You knew...this morning...that I wasn't Tania,' she
accused, the colour deepening in her cheeks. 'And yet
you still...'

'Purely out of curiosity, my dear child,' he interrupted coldly, 'to see whether or not you'd stop me.'

She stared at him, her fine, slender features appalled.
And it didn't help knowing that she had only herself to
blame for his derogatory opinion of her.

'Of course I'd have stopped you,' she uttered tremulously, wanting to convince him even if she couldn't
fully convince herself.

'Exactly when?' His tone was censuring. 'When I was so out of control it would have caused embarrassment to both of us? Do you enjoy teasing men, Romy Morgan? Misleading them into thinking they've got a chance...'

'No!' Her head lifted rebelliously, soft, blonde strands drying around her face. 'You can think whatever you like...'

'And what about Danny Gower?' A vein pumped spasmodically in Aaron's temple beneath the deep, Pacific tan. 'Has he been lucky enough to sample some of your generosity as well?'

Only the crack which sang through the air made Romy shamefully aware that she had struck him. Horrified, she watched the reddening patch forming on his cheek, her smarting hand against her mouth. She had never slapped a man in her life before—didn't know how she could have lost control to such a degree. But Aaron Blake, she realised hopelessly, was bringing out a passionate side to her nature she hadn't known existed.

The amber eyes probed hers. 'I see,' he said, quietly and coolly, remarkably coolly after such an assault, 'so it's just me you've chosen to honour with your favours.'

Shame burned her cheeks, and she stiffened, aware of the sensual undertones in his remark. He was so close to her that she could feel the warmth emanating from him—smell the tantalising spice of the cologne he had used.

Dear God, don't let him touch me, she begged silently, knowing that it wouldn't take too much effort on Aaron's part to discover that he was right. His opinion of her was low enough as it was, without being considered an easy lay as well. And for some reason, what he thought about her mattered a great deal.

She relaxed as he moved away to the poolside table, pouring himself some pineapple juice from the jug which a maid had brought out earlier.

'What really made you decide to come here, Romy?' His voice drifted across to her as he put down his glass—

soft, almost persuasive. 'And why couldn't Tania come herself?'

'I told you, I ...'

'The truth,' he insisted as if he knew she hadn't been completely open with him. 'Remember ... we're playing it straight now.'

A bee was hovering over the flame of an hibiscus, its outline blurred—indistinct, and Romy blinked several times, trying to focus upon it.

'Tania had an assignment she couldn't turn down,' she answered him, twisting his handkerchief mercilessly in her hands. 'It could lead to work in America which she's always wanted, but she didn't want to lose the house and she said she would if she wasn't seen to be using it. She looked so strained ... in need of a holiday,' Romy stated, remembering how her twin's appearance had caused her some concern, 'that I had to help her. And anyway, I ... I needed to get away.'

Subduedly, she studied her painted nails, discovering that the pain of losing her father wasn't quite so intense as it had been before. She shrugged, her shoulders a satiny gold against the scarlet strings of the bikini.

'I wanted to tell you ... more than once ... but I was afraid it would cost Tania her tenancy.' Which it probably would now, she thought, resignedly.

'Is that why you're dissecting my handkerchief?' He retrieved it from her agitated hands, his fingers accidentally grazing hers, causing her to flinch. 'Or is it in your plans to knit me another?'

She couldn't meet the mockery she knew was in his eyes, her heart beating too hard from that unexpected contact, and to put some space between them she went over to stand by the pool, staring down into its clear, turquoise depths.

'I'm leaving tomorrow, anyway,' she admitted, almost ruefully, without looking at him. 'So you can tell Theo what you like. I've already booked the flight.'

'Cancel it.'

She swung round, her eyes surprised yet mutinous—rebelling against the arrogance of his command. But his expression was inexorable, his mouth unmistakably determined.

'You aren't going to get off that lightly,' he assured her with a silky softness.

'W-what do you mean?' she queried uneasily, and took a step back as he moved towards her.

'What were you planning to do when you took off so unexpectedly tomorrow?' he demanded, without answering her. 'Leave a note to say your sister was sick and you just *had* to get home?'

The accuracy of his guess made her stiffen. Because wasn't that exactly what she had been considering?

The sun made her hair shine almost silver as she tilted her head, biting her lower lip.

'Something like that.'

Aaron's mouth pulled down one side. 'So it was just as well I forgot some papers and came back, wasn't it?' he remarked with hard derision. 'And I'm going to see to it that you serve a very useful purpose while you're here.'

'Exactly what does that mean?' she challenged brittly, trying not to feel threatened by the authority in his stance—legs slightly apart, his fists against the lean angle of his hips.

The dark features were taut, unrelenting. 'You came here as a favour to your sister... and by heaven! you're going to do her one,' he breathed. 'Starting with Sandra Donnington's party tonight!' He stared at her, his eyes darkening. 'As it would appear that your sister's having an affair...'

'What's that got to do with me?' she snapped angrily, through revulsion in imagining Tania with another woman's husband. Over the breeze which sang through the cypress tree, Aaron's voice was decisively cool.

'Everything... since you've chosen to take her place.' He moved closer to her but she stood her ground. 'When Tania was here last time she wasn't particularly dis-

creet—a gift from the gods for a man like Quintin Swain.'
The amber eyes were hard, and there was a flush of
colour on the strong cheekbones. 'I had virtually to
threaten to knock his brains out to stop him printing a
nice juicy story...to keep Tania from being scandalised
from here to Antarctica!' His mouth tightened. 'Well,
he'll be at that party tonight, Romy, since it's to pub-
licise the launch of a new company more than a social
affair. Him, and a host of others who saw your sister
with Gower last time...and since *he's* going too, so are
you...*as* your sister. Only tonight you're going to put
up a very good display of showing everyone where Tania
Morgan's affections really lie...with me!'

'No!' Stunned by what he was suggesting, she stepped
back and would have toppled into the pool if he hadn't
had the razor-sharp reflexes to grab her. With his arm
around her midriff, she felt every nerve leap into startling life, the fine material of his suit such a sensual experience against her almost naked body, that her head
swam.

'Let me go,' she murmured shakily.

He didn't at first, catching her against him as if he
wanted to prolong the intimacy. As if he were going to
kiss her! she thought wildly, her racing heart causing her
breasts to rise sharply beneath the naked desire in his
eyes. But then he was releasing her, leaving her feeling
oddly bereft as he stepped back, all traces of emotion
gone.

Of course. He didn't have to pretend any more, either.

'Well?' he said.

Romy looked at him broodingly, at a wall of determination she didn't know how to break down. He was
asking her to spend the evening as Tania...not only in
front of a man her sister was supposed to be having an
affair with, but also in view of the Press. And there
would be others there too, he'd said, who knew about
her sister and Danny Gower, so that there would
probably be whispers behind her back...curious glances,
she thought, cringing. But the most disconcerting thing,

she realised with a shudder, was having to pretend that she was emotionally involved with Aaron Blake. How could she when he affected her so much? When she knew she couldn't possibly play a part like that non-committally?

'You can't make me do it,' she tossed up at him, her mouth tightening defiantly.

His own compressed. 'True,' he stated, which brought a spark of surprise to her eyes. 'But I think you care enough about your sister to want to help save her reputation. Gower's a top Government official here. A sordid scandal could ruin his career...not that that bothers me particularly. But it *could* harm Tania's, and I'm sure you wouldn't want that. Oh, and of course, you'll be preventing Theo from selling the house. It's up to you.'

Which was blackmail, she thought. Pure and simple.

Disdainfully, she moved away from him, watching the bee which had left the vivid hibiscus for the yielding pollens of the gardenias. She was having difficulty focusing and felt a twinge of pain above her left eye.

Really, he gave her no choice, she reflected, annoyed by how he was turning this deception to his own advantage. She wasn't sure whether he would actually tell his cousin if she didn't comply. He obviously cared a lot about Tania to go to such drastic lengths to protect her reputation, she decided, experiencing a stab of some emotion she couldn't quite define. So perhaps his threat about the house had very little substance. But he *was* right. She loved her twin too much to turn her back on her when her name could be defiled—perhaps her career jeopardised—no matter how foolish her sister had been. And Aaron was using that love, knowing that she couldn't go home without trying to help her twin, regardless of how embarrassing that might prove to be.

'All right,' she sighed, defeatedly, turning back to him. 'I'll do as you say.'

'Good.'

A small pulse beat hard in her throat as he came closer, and she saw his eyes move to it and rest there—slightly mocking, aware.

'In return, you can stay here for the rest of your holiday as planned...get on with whatever writing you want to do...as long as you abide by the rules...go where I take you...and nip any malicious gossip in the bud once and for all.'

She had to keep up this charade for the whole month? Go along with his plans, pretending to everyone that he was her lover?

Her throat constricting, she wanted to protest. She couldn't face these unsettling feelings he evoked in her whenever she was with him. But she supposed she would have to if she wanted to stop any gossip about Tania, and that meant far more to her than protecting a simple tenancy as she had come here initially to do.

Wearily, she nodded her acceptance, feeling slightly sick. Something was wrong, and she had only just realised what it was.

'What's the matter?' he asked, quick to notice.

'I've lost one of my contacts.'

Disbelief etched the strong features. 'You mean...you wear lenses?'

Another point against her, she thought despairingly, adding for good measure, 'Glasses, usually.'

'Well, well. You're a bundle of surprises, aren't you? What are you suggesting I do?' His tone was abrasive. 'Drain the pool?'

'Of course not,' she shot back. And not wanting to appear a complete fool, 'I don't normally swim in them, only I didn't think...'

'I wonder why,' he drawled sarcastically, obviously guessing at the way she must have plunged back in without thinking as soon as she had thought he'd gone. 'I take it you've a spare?'

Sheepishly, she shook her head, feeling even more like an idiot when she heard his whispered expletive, until it dawned what losing the lens would mean.

'I won't be able to do what you wanted me to now, will I?'

She couldn't very well pretend to be Tania if she was wearing glasses, could she? she thought, immeasurably relieved that she wouldn't have to play that disconcerting role after all.

'Oh yes, you will.' Aaron's resolution was as swift as it was grim. 'You'll be attending that party tonight if I have to lead you by the hand every step of the way, so get used to the idea.'

He was intent on protecting Tania's reputation at any cost, Romy realised. Which could only mean that he loved her twin very much. And goodness knew! she thought, with that same stab of indefinable emotion piercing her, she wanted to keep the Press from writing anything sordid about Tania—perhaps even more than Aaron did. They were sisters, after all! But the fact that he could do it, without any regard for *her* at all, hit hard.

'That won't be necessary... I'm not *totally* blind,' she delivered cuttingly, and swung away from him, hiding the hurt in her eyes as she went back inside to change.

Sandra Donnington's house was over an hour's drive away, and Romy's nervous tension mounted until it was coiling like a spring inside of her when Aaron handed her out of the Ferrari.

'Nervous?'

She was as aware of the mockery in his voice as of his fingers curling around her elbow and, irritated, she pulled away from him, only to grasp at his arm when she almost tripped over a step owing to limited vision.

'You started this little game,' he reminded her softly, his breath fanning her hair, and it was no consolation to admit to herself that he was right.

'Tania, darling! How lovely to see you again.'

Romy recognised the lively, feminine voice from the telephone the day before and she clutched Aaron's arm more tightly, tension building to an almost sickening pain

in her stomach. She noticed the glance he shot her way—
thought he looked half amused, as far as her blurred
vision would permit her to judge—but she ignored it,
drawing in a deep breath as their hostess came up to
them.

Sandra Donnington was a middle-aged woman who
obviously took great pains with her appearance, Romy
deduced, noting the stylish black dress which enhanced
her slim figure and set off the well groomed fair hair.
A widow, whose husband had made his fortune with a
revolutionary air-cooling system, she remembered Aaron
telling her on the way over. And not only the richest
woman on the island, but a very old friend. The way
she kissed him on the cheek and then hugged him for a
long moment confirmed it, the gesture tugging at Romy's
heart.

'I see you've secured yourself the best-looking escort
in Viti!' the woman was complimenting her. 'And if I
were you I'd stamp my name on him before someone
else does!'

She was laughing, but Romy couldn't help wondering
if it was a subtle suggestion that her sister kept away
from ineligible men like Danny Gower. If it was, then
it was meant in the kindest possible way, she decided,
because the vibes she picked up from Sandra Donnington were of warmth and sincerity.

'You're looking lovelier than ever,' she smiled with
matronly generosity. 'But what have you been doing with
yourself since we saw you last? You'll have to tell me
all about it. We'll have a long chat later on if Aaron can
bear to let you go. And what a beautiful dress!'

Romy responded equally warmly, telling herself that
the chances of saying anything out of place in front of
her hostess were very slim. She'd be lucky to get a word
in edgeways! she thought fondly—relieved—and stole a
little confidence from the woman's approval of her dress.
She had bought it that afternoon, having brought
nothing from Melbourne suitable for such a party, and
the odd one or two gowns in Tania's wardrobe not having

appealed. Aaron had driven her into town, leaving her
to shop while he attended a business meeting, but she
hadn't had to look far. She had fallen in love with the
dress the instant she'd seen it—a gown of scarlet silk
with a plunging neckline and soft, swirling skirt which
emphasised the pure gold of her hair, and made her feel
uncustomarily daring. Aaron had been impressed, she
thought, when he'd picked her up tonight, his gaze
running appreciatively over the soft, swept-back hair,the
subtle effects of her make-up, down over the slender lines
of her body, before coming to rest on the tantalising
valley of her breasts with such unveiled sensuality that
she had blushed. He'd even said she looked beautiful.
And she'd known a surge of warmth in having pleased
him, until her cool inner self ridiculed the little burst of
joy she'd felt, chilling her with the truth. Of course he
approved. She looked exactly like Tania.

Telling herself not to be foolish enough to forget that,
she allowed him to lead her into the old, colonial
mansion, steeling herself for the awkward hours ahead.

It was obvious that Aaron would attract attention—
particularly from the female guests, she thought, as heads
immediately turned their way. He was dynamic enough
without the additional elegance of a blue velvet dinner-
jacket and dark trousers, but with a small tremor she
realised that their interest was distributed equally between her escort and herself, and she supposed that any
woman to have accompanied him would have aroused
natural curiosity, even without her being someone they
thought was an Australian celebrity. She shivered, wondering how she was ever going to pull this thing off.

'Just smile that Mona Lisa smile of yours and no one
will know the difference,' he advised in a low voice,
turning immediately to address someone with a superb
confidence Romy envied.

The evening was a nightmare. People kept milling
round them—not necessarily friends, she deduced at
some stage, but young men eager to know Aaron—
probably hopeful that his influence might further their

careers—and women who just wanted to talk to him.
And there were those who wanted to be seen socialising
with Tania Morgan, so Romy wore a smile for the ben-
efit of everyone until her jaw ached, conscious only of
that strong arm around her waist—of Aaron's determination to show all these people that Tania was his.

She was nursing a feeling remarkably akin to jealousy,
trying to ignore the heat of his hand through her dress,
when she was mortified to find herself standing next to
some producer with whom her twin had worked, and
she tensed as he asked her a question only Tania could
have answered.

She pressed her lips together, feeling Aaron's eyes upon
her, even though he was apparently talking to someone
else. He wouldn't like it if she made some careless
mistake.

'It's a lovely party,' she was responding to the man
beside her with a flutter of her lashes. 'Don't let's spoil
the night by talking shop.'

It worked. The man gave a grunt of acquiescence and
disappeared, leaving Romy sighing relief.

'Well done. You handled that with positive finesse.'

Above the strains of a moody melody, Aaron's approval was threaded with mockery, and Romy's hackles
rose.

'Don't worry... I shan't spoil your little game,' she
uttered curtly, her eyes glittering with anger and frustration from those few embarrassing moments. She
wouldn't be in this position if it weren't for him!

And he must have realised that—determined though
he'd seemed to make her pay for deceiving him—because he stayed close to her, helping her out of any
further awkward situations which arose, with admirable
coolness. That was, until a vivacious brunette suddenly
linked arms with him, and murmuring something to
Romy about keeping him all to herself, drew him away,
and what little confidence she had had while he was at
her side, instantly melted.

What would she do now? With a dry throat she darted a glance across the groups of indistinct faces—a hot, clammy feeling creeping over her. Still, if she ignored people she was supposed to know, what did it matter? she thought with a suddenly fey attitude. She couldn't see them properly, anyway!

'Come on... drink up.' Sandra was offering her more champagne but Romy smilingly declined it.

'I like to keep a clear head,' she said without thinking, and could have kicked herself. Tania's limit was hardly two glasses! But if her hostess thought she was behaving out of character, she was too polite to say so.

'Is it easy... keeping a clear head when a man like Aaron's driving you home?'

Ridiculously, Romy blushed. Perhaps that was why she needed to, she thought, because when he was near she felt heady enough without any alcohol.

'You like him a lot, don't you?' she felt compelled to say, and Sandra nodded.

'Like the brother I never had.' Blue eyes smiled warmly. 'Though I warn you now...if I were a few years younger, Tania, you'd have some competition from this quarter! Oh damn!' Romy looked up questioningly as the woman shot a glance across the room. 'The Press have arrived, and so has that distasteful freelance character, Quintin Swain. I was hoping he'd stay away. Aaron won't be at all pleased... well, you know how much he hates the Press anyway, let alone a man like that.'

Romy's gaze followed the older woman's to the blond man who was looking around him with shrewd, lashless eyes, and supposed that a party given by the richest woman on the island—for whatever reason—would be the perfect source of gossip for a man like Swain. A chill ran through her as she remembered how irritating and unpleasant she had found him on the plane and on the beach that day. And now she knew why Aaron had acted as he had—because the man had wanted a scoop about her sister and Danny. But she sensed that that wasn't

the only reason for Aaron's attitude towards
newspapermen.

'I know he's never liked them,' she came out with gingerly, trying to sound as though she'd known him longer
than three days. 'But he's never told me why.'

'Hasn't he?' Sandra sounded surprised. 'I believe it
has something to do with his mother. Why don't you
ask him?' she suggested, reluctantly excusing herself to
organise the photographs of her new company's
directors.

'Waiting for me?' The smooth, male voice cut across
the lively tempo being played before Romy could even
consider what Sandra had said, and she swung around,
her body stiffening as she looked up into the leering face
of Danny Gower. His bow-tie was slightly askew, and
even in a dark evening suit he was without any of the
elegance which was so inherent in Aaron.

'Actually, I wasn't,' she answered coolly, and turned
heavily shaded lids away, ostensibly to watch the blurred,
bobbing figures in the middle of the floor though she
was searching frantically for Aaron. Why didn't he come
back?

'You seem to have been abandoned, which is a perfect
stroke of luck for me,' Danny remarked in a suggestive
way Romy didn't like. 'Why don't we go out into the
garden and get some air...spend some time alone?
There's a lovely moon out there tonight.'

Romy darted a cold look at him, meeting the indistinct features which she sensed were hungry for an affair,
and guessing that this sort of philandering came as
second nature to him. How on earth had Tania got
herself involved with a man like this? she wondered
again, unhappily.

'What a lovely idea.' Suddenly she was responding to
his invitation with a generous smile. 'And is your wife
coming, too?'

She felt, rather than saw the way he recoiled from her
caustic taunt because her ineffectual eyes were scanning
the room again for some sign of Aaron.

'What the hell's wrong with you this time? You weren't like this before.' It was a hissed rebuke from Danny as Romy tried to make out the dark, commanding figure of the man who had brought her here, her lovely face lined with tension. 'Blake's probably in an intimate clinch somewhere with that brunette I saw him with just now,' the man commented, obviously noting her anxious glances around the room. 'So why don't we follow their example?' His fingers ran down her arm, making her flinch. 'Come on...let yourself go.'

'Why don't you? Preferably back to the woman you married!'

The retort escaped her before she could stop it, the thought of this man making love to her twin already sickening her, but that last remark about Aaron and the brunette had been the final straw.

'Jealous because your rich boyfriend fancies someone else?' he jeered nastily, and Romy felt a stab of something under her ribs.

Of course she wasn't jealous, she tried convincing herself. She was just annoyed that he should have dragged her here as Tania tonight, when he obviously wanted to be with anyone rather than *her*. And she had let her temper flare because of it. Whatever was happening to her? she wondered self-chidingly. What did it matter to her who Aaron was with? What he did? Until a few days ago she hadn't even known he existed.

'I've just simply no intention of getting involved with a married man,' she said waspishly, and from a few feet away suddenly noticed Quintin Swain watching them interestedly. She couldn't see his expression. But as Danny moved to catch her wrist, she saw the indistinct action of a camera lift menacingly and knew that she had to get away! And suddenly hard fingers were closing around her forearm. She was being jerked aside. And as an electronic flash caught an astounded-looking Government official, she heard a deep, authoritative voice suggest, 'All right, Gower...you heard what the lady said. Get back to your domestic bliss.'

Romy didn't see him go, only aware of Aaron's arms tightening relentlessly around her. Her hands resting rather tentatively against the soft velvet of his jacket, she thought how fresh he smelt—how pleasantly male— his cologne elusive and subtle after the rather sickly aftershave lotion the other man had been wearing.

'It looks like I moved in just in time, doesn't it?' he said, grazingly, pulling her into the throng of dancing couples. 'Another second and you could have been appearing in tomorrow's newspapers. Or is that what you want?' The amber eyes scrutinised her coldly. 'Perhaps your sister put you up to getting yourself featured with Gower, because you're certainly going the right way about it. First in his car. And now here, where you knew Swain would be.'

Romy looked up at him mutinously. 'For your information, Aaron Blake, I can't stand the man.' Relief, which had been so immense when he'd rescued her just now was wearing off, leaving her disconcerted—a reluctant prisoner in his arms. 'I didn't know who he was when he gave me a lift that day. And as for getting myself in the papers...you didn't seem to worry too much about that when you went off and left me to cope by myself,' she accused brittly, finding anger the only possible source of defence against the sensations his nearness was producing in her.

'I didn't *go off*, as you put it. I was with a couple of business colleagues just behind you,' he returned, smoothly, his breath fanning her cheek. 'And I'm sure you didn't need me to put on a perfect deception without turning a hair.' His words flayed like a silken whip. 'Unless, of course, you're trying to tell me you missed me...'

There was cool laughter in his eyes, and she had to look away, feeling the colour creeping up her throat.

Well, at least he hadn't been in an intimate clinch with the brunette!

Shocked to realise how much comfort there was in knowing that, as the last note of the music faded she started to pull away, only to discover that he wasn't prepared to let her go.

'Stay here,' he commanded softly.

A dreamy number was beginning—the lights were suddenly dimmed—and he was pulling her closer to him, causing a warm tide of desire to flood through her veins. Against her bare skin, the velvet was sensuous, making her catch her breath, and the way Aaron was looking at her, his eyes darkly slumbrous, assured her that he was as aware of her as she was of him.

'Put your arms around me.'

She had been holding back, conscious of how intimately the other couples were dancing, and, gingerly now, she slid her hands up over his jacket, to clasp them at the nape of his neck. His hair felt coarse and strong beneath her fingers so that she couldn't stop them luxuriating in an innocently provocative caress of the dark strands.

She heard his deep groan of satisfaction and every cell in her body tensed. Of course! He wanted the world to see that he was Tania's lover. Tania's—not yours, she assured herself firmly, the harsh reality that he would rather be holding her sister causing her to draw back.

'What's wrong?' he breathed, his expression darkly puzzling. 'Anyone would think you didn't want to be in my arms.'

'Then they're right—I don't,' she uttered tartly, pulling away, but his strength was enveloping her mercilessly.

'That wasn't the impression I got in the swimming pool this morning...or after dinner last night.' His voice was low, dangerously soft. 'So let's not pretend any more, shall we?'

This close to him she could see the cool derision in his eyes. Her cheeks flamed and a small pulse beat furiously in her throat, betraying her.

'See,' he mocked lightly, his hand sliding down until his thumb was resting against the small, throbbing hollow. And with his lips gently teasing hers, 'You want me . . .'

She would have denied it, but the sensuality of his mouth as it tormented hers with light kisses made her breathless with its promise of the greater intimacy she craved.

And suddenly it was covering hers, and with such devastation to her senses that she could only cling to him and submit to his will, a soft yelp escaping her as he caught her hard against him. She could feel the heat of his body burning through the red silk—realised how aroused he was—and all she could think was that she wanted to be closer to him—to be naked in his arms and know the hard dominance of his possession, the reckless thought making her move sensuously against him, oblivious to everyone else around them.

'Easy,' he whispered gently, relaxing his hold, and she gave an involuntary little protest, only after a moment realising that the music had stopped.

As the lights went up she thought he looked flushed—noticed that his breathing was as ragged as hers.

'What did I do to deserve that?'

He sounded amused, and in the brighter atmosphere—standing apart from him now—she felt thoroughly ashamed.

What could she say? I wanted you to kiss me and I got carried away when you did? What would he make of that? He already thought she was wanton after her behaviour in the pool today.

'You wanted a performance, didn't you?' she hissed at him, embarrassment adding acidity to her voice. 'Well, you got one . . . now take me home.'

Strangely, he complied almost at once, and they drove in total silence for most of the way.

Danny had been right, she noticed, her gaze fixed numbly on the windscreen. A big, beautiful moon was making its slow ascent into the inky sky, lending an ephemeral magic to the Fijian night. Aaron's window was open and she could smell the salty air—hear the wash of the ocean as it broke on some quiet, deserted beach.

A place like the rest of the world should be, she remembered some holiday brochure describing Fiji. A place to lose your heart. And, intuitively, she knew in that moment that she should never have come.

'Romy.'

She looked at him from under her lashes as he spoke to her—met that dark, commanding profile with a flutter in her stomach.

'I make no apologies for what happened back there. You're a very desirable girl.' His eyes were coolly appraising. 'But for what it's worth...I didn't intend to let things go that far.'

And that solved everything!

With a swish of blonde hair, Romy turned away, her expression pained. It didn't do much for her ego to know that she could turn him on because she looked like Tania.

'Why worry?' She gave a brittle laugh, sounding more like her twin than herself. 'Everybody probably thinks we're having a mad, passionate affair now. That was the idea, wasn't it?'

She felt his cursory glance across the car's dark interior.

'Was that all it was...a big act?'

His contempt was tangible, and Romy bit down hard on her lower lip. Let him believe it if he wanted to! It was less humiliating than telling him that, physically, she couldn't resist him.

'What else?' she lied, with an effusive sweep of her hand, and only then considered how much he must think she was behaving like Tania.

'My God, you're cool.' She felt the censuring lash of his tongue which confirmed it and she shivered as he looked away from her, back to the road.

Why, oh why did she have to be so attracted to a man who was in love with her sister? A man who obviously thought she was promiscuous as well as deceitful and clearly despised her because of it. She wished she were home—anywhere but in this car with him—and was relieved when he pulled up outside the house.

He came round to open her door—courteous to the last—and, muttering a hasty goodnight, Romy brushed past him, her heart seeming to stand still as he caught her wrist, turning her round in his arms.

The red silk rustled as she twisted to get away from him, trying to ignore the feel of the fine shirt beneath her fingers, that familiar male scent of him, and she stiffened. If she succumbed to him now he would know that it hadn't been an act back there, and she wasn't ready to admit, even to herself, why she'd behaved as she had, both at that party and in his pool today.

'Resistance, Romy?' The deep voice mocked her— testing her immunity to him—and it took all her will to fight the ecstasy of his lips against her throat.

'There's no one about…we don't have to pretend any more,' she bit out icily, tugging away, and caught the briefest glimpse of the cloud which crossed his face before she tore up the steps.

And later, in bed, with the moonlight silhouetting the wood-carving in a hideous distortion of a girl and her shadow, tears came.

CHAPTER SIX

ROMY didn't see Aaron again for the next couple of days, and was annoyed with herself for experiencing an absurd disappointment.

Why should it matter to her? she asked herself logically. She had no more interest in him than he had in her. In fact, she was only seeing him for Tania's sake, she reminded herself half chidingly, and, determined to put him firmly to the back of her mind, absorbed herself in her writing, grateful that she could at least wear her glasses now that she was alone. When she went out, as when Aaron had driven her into Suva to buy the dress, she could clip her sun-lenses to them, but naturally, indoors when Niki was around, or if she went out at night, that wouldn't do. She would have to try and get a replacement lens, she thought vaguely, becoming more engrossed in her work; it wasn't until she put down her pen that night that she realised that not only had she recaptured her old form, but that her writing seemed to surpass anything she'd done before. And with a contented sigh, she switched off the light and went to bed.

A movement in her room woke her. Opening her eyes, she gasped, seeing a tall figure standing by her bed.

'Ssh!' Immediately a hand was covering her mouth, though it wouldn't have mattered if she had cried out because no one would have heard, she thought, when she'd recovered from her initial shock. She stared up at Aaron through the half-light, now fully awake.

'What are you doing here?' she breathed, flabbergasted, when he allowed her to speak. 'How did you get in?'

It was barely dawn, which didn't help her at all in trying to make out his expression.

'It wasn't hard getting hold of a key.'

'Why?' Like him, she was whispering as though the early hour was somehow sacred. 'What do you want?'

'Sweet revenge?'

Romy's heart skipped a beat. 'What for?' she asked warily, drawing herself up to lean on an elbow. And guessed, as she sensed the sardonic lift of a thick, dark eyebrow. She'd made him look a fool by deceiving him, hadn't she? And somehow she suspected that men like Aaron Blake didn't take very kindly to being deluded.

She cast her tongue nervously over her dry lips. 'I thought you'd already had that,' she said, shakily, because his cool fingers had slipped beneath the short fall of blonde hair, massaging the sensitive skin with an amazingly sensual skill. 'The other night...the party...'

Hampered by poor sight and the dimness of the room, she wasn't certain, but she thought he smirked.

'That was for someone else. *This*...is personal.'

She wanted to ask what he meant but her breathing came too fast as his hand slid down to the strap of her shortie-nightie, slipping it off her shoulder, and her mouth went dry. He laughed softly at the rebellion in her eyes.

'Get dressed.'

'What?' That was the last thing she had expected, and she heard him laugh again at her surprise.

'Of course, if you'd rather not...'

'All right!'

As he reached for the other strap she was jumping out of bed, deciding she was less vulnerable on her feet, although when she saw the insolent way in which he was appreciating her long, bare legs and her body beneath the clinging material, she wasn't so sure.

'Do you always make a point of walking into ladies' bedrooms uninvited?' she asked, darting him a scathing glance as she reached for her clothes.

'No, it's usually by invitation.' There was a note of dry humour in his voice, and glancing at him again—at his perfect, denim-clad physique and that dark, unquestionable magnestism—she could believe it. A tug of excitement made itself felt, which she did her best to ignore.

'Just what do you think you've got in mind?' she queried, heatedly, clutching her clothes to her and wondering, rather uneasily, if he intended staying there.

'You'll find out.'

A man of few words! she thought, grimly. But at least he had the courtesy to wait outside while she dressed.

She was joining him in minutes, in jeans and a white T-shirt, with only the large-framed glasses accentuating the almond-shaped eyes.

He grimaced when he saw her.

'So this is the real Romy Morgan,' he drawled, seemingly amused, but he didn't say whether he approved. How could he?

'Come on.'

He was holding the door open for her—letting in the early-morning air—but Romy stayed exactly where she was, bristling from his audacity—the way he was ordering her about. Outside, she heard some bird whistle, its note shrill and distinct—caught the stirring perfume of the frangipani.

'Give me one good reason why I should?' she demanded, her eyes glittering with a challenge.

He came back to her slowly, purposefully, the power of his shoulders and thighs emphasised by the blue denim.

'An interested buyer for this property?' he suggested, without a flicker of compunction, and Romy shivered.

'You'd still tell Theo?' She couldn't believe that he would. 'Why?' she queried, when his implacable expression assured her otherwise.

His shoulder lifted casually. 'Why not?'

Because you love Tania, she nearly said, but stopped herself in time. She couldn't be sure of that. Perhaps hard men like him didn't feel love—only desire. But he was angry with her twin because of Danny, and with *her* for misleading him, possibly angry enough to carry out his threat at the drop of a hat, she suspected, if she didn't co-operate with him.

'That's blackmail,' she accused reprovingly, shooting him a cold look as she brushed past him on to the veranda. 'It's low and despicable...'

'So is deceit.'

His chilling reminder sent a dart of remorse through her, and she could only respond with a sullen pout as he handed her into the Ferrari.

The barely risen sun was making the horizon gleam gold—a glittering promise of the hot day to come—and way above the blue water some sea-bird wheeled, its white wings a flash of silver as it turned, then swooped, in its eternal quest for fish.

'Where are we going?'

They were on an open road lined with coconut palms and mangrove, and Aaron was using almost full throttle, that superb self-confidence and male aggression reflected in the way he drove.

'You'll see.'

Romy glared at his rugged, inexorable profile, hating the way he had virtually abducted her—by refusing to tell her where he was taking her—but he didn't acknowledge her hard stare, which was even more infuriating, keeping his concentration on the road.

'You're really enjoying making me pay, aren't you?' she snapped, her hair a pale gold against the soft tan of her face.

He didn't look at her, casting a glance in his rear-view mirror with an amused curl to his lips.

'If on the dance floor last night was anything to go by, I'd say you weren't altogether averse to your punishment...despite your protestations, Romy.'

He looked at her then from under those enviably long lashes, the sagacity behind his smile chastening her, bringing warm colour to her cheeks. He was right, she thought abjectly, staring at the road coming towards them. Because though her mind wanted to deny it, her body responded traitorously whenever he touched her, and last night she had revelled in being in his arms. He had made her want him with a passion which even that first love affair had failed to awaken in her, and the humiliating thing was that he knew how little resistance she had where he was concerned. She had to hit out at him, if only verbally—say something to lessen this shame she was suffering at finding herself so ensnared by that powerful sensuality—and so, her voice tight from a bruised ego, she remarked, 'And I suppose you think you're an expert in human nature, Aaron Blake?'

He laughed softly, manoeuvring the car round a particularly dangerous bend.

'My dear girl, when you get to be my age you'll realise that it's only a fool who considers himself an expert in human nature. It's grossly diverse and thoroughly unpredictable, and the sooner one learns that lesson, the easier life is.'

Which was a typically cynical remark, Romy thought, glancing at him, and couldn't help wondering what his own life had dealt out to make him that way. In fact, there were a great many things she wanted to know about him. Like his background. His family. And what had happened with his mother to make him hate the Press.

'Why don't you ask him?' Sandra Donnington had said. But looking at the suddenly grim lines of that taut profile, Romy couldn't.

'Since I'm supposed to be Tania...wouldn't you prefer to have me with my make-up on?' she suggested curtly, after a moment, having brought it with her since he had allowed her no time to attend to it back at the house.

The hard mouth twitched. 'What makes you think I'm going to *have* you at all?' he drawled, so that she blushed furiously and looked away, wishing she had been more prudent in her choice of words. She felt him glance at her—long enough for him to notice the embarrassed colour in her cheeks with some amusement—and then

he turned away, saying dispassionately. 'You'll do ... for
what I have in mind.'

Which was a jaunt on his thirty-foot power cruiser,
as it turned out!

To ask where they were going would have been futile,
she sensed, watching with silent admiration as Aaron
steered the expensive vessel away from the yachts, cabin
cruisers and sailing dinghies in the marina with a long-
practised skill.

Away from the shore the air was fresher and Romy
slipped her hands under her hair to let the sea breeze
caress the nape of her neck, savouring the taste of salt
spray on her lips. She caught Aaron's eyes on her, travelling down to rest on the points of her breasts beneath
the T-shirt, and she let her arms fall, discomposed by
his blatant male scrutiny.

'Have you ever steered a boat?'

His question sent a little burst of excitement through
her.

'No.'

'Come here.'

She looked at him with her eyes shining in anticipation as he stood aside for her to take the helm, her
hands closing over the smooth, polished wood.

'Gently now ... that's better.'

His fingers were covering hers on the wheel—guiding
the boat —his voice instructive and steady, and Romy
felt her pulse start to race from his nearness—the strong,
hard control of his hand.

'I—I think I've got the idea,' she said shakily, hoping
he would move away, which, fortunately, he did after a
few moments.

'That's right ... now let her have some headway.' His
voice came to her across the sound of the engine—
through the vigorous embrace of the wind. 'She'll do
thirty knots top speed.'

Romy wasn't too well acquainted with nautical terms
but knew enough to realise that that was fast, and she
felt the thrust of power as they cruised out into the vast

expanse of blue water, leaving a stream of turbulent, white foam in their wake.

'Over there's Bèqa,' Aaron was pointing out, 'and in that direction... Toberua and Gau.'

Romy smiled, envying his knowledge of the islands.

'How long have you lived here?' she asked, her desire to know more about him getting the better of her.

'About seven years.'

She shot a glance at him. He was looking at a sailing dinghy through some binoculars—more like the captain of some pirate ship with his rugged, dark looks, she fantasised, instead of a thriving businessman taking a few hours off to relax.

'And before that... New Zealand?'

He nodded.

'Which part?' she asked curiously.

Strong brown hands held the binoculars steady. 'The South Island.'

'What made you leave?'

'There was nothing for me there.' His tone was suddenly abrupt and, laying the binoculars down, he came and took over the helm. 'After I left university I joined Theo and his wife in the North Island for a while. And if you're wondering about the age difference between my cousin and me,' he interjected, surprising her because she had been, 'it's something to do with being once removed. He taught me all I know about property development,' he went on, 'so I came here and started in business on my own.'

And very successfully, too, Romy couldn't help adding silently.

'Why Fiji?' she queried, admiring him for his capability—that endurable strength and determination only a few rare men, like him, possessed to take them to the top. 'Why Viti Levu?'

'A desire to get away from the crowd.'

'Only that?' she laughed, her eyes wide—curious—behind the large frames. She hadn't imagined that a man who would attract attention wherever he went would share her liking for seclusion.

'And a need to try and ensure that the natural beauty of these islands isn't spoilt by unsympathetic development. With my money and my line of work I can do that,' he told her. 'Which is much more satisfying and beneficial than building concrete jungles on the mainland.'

She could see his point, though until a few days ago, she wouldn't have thought a man like him would care.

'So you do work?' she said impishly, pushing her hair back from her face. Her skin felt damp and cool.

'Yes...and damn hard.' There was a teasing reprimand in the glittering amber eyes as the vessel sliced its way through the warm, Pacific waters. 'But I also play hard, too, when I get the opportunity.'

She could believe that. From what she knew of him already she guessed that he would expect the very best out of life—and get it. But he would give his own best in return, she knew instinctively, and the thought sent a strange tingle through her.

Way back, a gentle mist obscured the coastline, while further out the chrome of moored yachts threw back dazzling reflections from the now fully risen sun.

'What about your parents?' He hadn't said anything about them and she wondered why. And couldn't help feeling as though she were prying as she added, tentatively, 'Are—are they still alive?'

Tense lines etched the strong features. 'I suppose my father is...somewhere. He was a barrister, believe it or not. Very clever...and very intolerant of a wife and small son, although I suppose we were good for his image...the respectable family man.' Aaron's tone was harshly mocking. 'That was until he was rather indiscreet with a teenage beauty queen and, with them both being newsworthy people, the papers had a field day. The story was all over London before my mother even suspected the affair. When she knew, she couldn't take it.' His mouth pulled down one side, and Romy noticed the whites of his knuckles as he gripped the helm. 'She went out that night and put her car over a bridge.'

Romy shuddered violently, noting the desolation in the deep voice.

'I'm sorry,' she whispered. And thought how futile that sounded.

'After that,' she heard him saying, his voice surprisingly controlled now, 'my father married his little beauty queen and I was parcelled off to various aunts and boarding schools because she couldn't tolerate children any more than he could. So that's my life…in a nutshell.'

She wanted to put her arms around him and comfort him—soothe his pain and bitterness brought about by a childhood so different from the loving security of her own—but he seemed too aloof and she held back, concern in her eyes. But she couldn't help feeling angry as she considered how a thoughtless teenager and someone intent on a story had contributed to an innocent woman killing herself; then realised with a sickening revulsion that Tania was doing exactly the same thing as that other girl—breaking up a marriage. No wonder Aaron had been so angry towards her when he had thought she was Tania, Romy reasoned, feeling the wind in her hair—the sun on her bare arms—without really being aware of it. He could probably see the same thing happening all over again, since Danny was very influential…

'Does Danny have any children?'

The question was out before she could stop it and she saw Aaron's eyes flicker over her, cognisant, yet darkly pained.

'Yes.' He breathed deeply, glancing seawards again. 'He has a seven year-old daughter.'

'I see,' Romy responded, softly. And she did. Now she could understand why he was so cynical. Why he'd acted as he had towards Quintin Swain the other day. Why he hated the Press. What had happened in his childhood could affect *anyone* for life. So perhaps…

Her breathing quickened with a surge of rash hope. Perhaps it wasn't just jealousy which had motivated him into trying to convince everyone that he was still Tania's lover. Perhaps...

'Did you bring a swimsuit?'

She was so deep in her thoughts she hadn't realised that he had cut the engine.

'If you didn't, I took the liberty of bringing the one you left drying on the terrace...'

'No, it's all right.' Reluctantly, she dragged her mind back to reality, telling herself firmly that to harbour any false hopes about Aaron Blake and herself could only lead to unhappiness—hers. She was under no illusion that he would ever want her for herself. And after those embarrassing moments when he'd been driving her up to his house the other day, she'd been determined this morning not to take any chances, stuffing a bikini into her bag before they'd left. 'I brought one with me,' she told him, wondering if it was his intention to sunbathe for a while.

'Then go and change,' was all he said.

He was waiting for her when she came up from below, leaning back against the rail looking like a bronze god in nothing but the dark trunks with the contrasting blue of the sky and the sea behind him, and Romy coloured when she saw the way his eyes raked over her near-naked figure.

'You'll need these,' he said, handing her some goggles. 'I'm going to show you some of the island's best-kept secrets.'

Underwater!

Excitement threaded through her veins, and she knew a wild exhilaration a few moments later when she took a deep breath and plunged down after him into the warm sea.

The water was so clear, she swore she could see down a hundred feet. A little way ahead, Aaron was leading the way, his powerful, lithe physique as graceful as it was strong. Romy followed him, revelling in the freedom of the ocean. Beautiful, treacherous coral spanned the silent, underwater world—a vivid red and blue near the surface, changing to a hard, dense black much further down. Inquisitive, coral-reef fish nosed their way towards them and turned away, unperturbed by their presence, and a small turtle paddled out from the looming darkness of a cave.

Romy surfaced to take air, and saw Aaron do the same. Laughing, she twisted away before he could speak to her, plunging down again, unable to get enough of that secret, marine world. The waving fronds of some exquisite plant beckoned her. She moved towards it and saw Aaron approaching swiftly, gesturing to her to keep away.

He was used to all this, she realised enviously, marvelling at the breathtaking structure of the coral. He would know which plants were dangerous, which were not. Know, too, when the currents were right to dive. Which was probably why they had left so early, she thought, on reflection.

'Why did you bring me?' she asked when they were on the sun-deck a little later, stretched out in the intensifying heat. After all, there wasn't anyone around to see them together, so he had nothing to gain by bringing her out here today.

His lips compressed. 'Because you got more than you bargained for by coming here, Romy Morgan. And though I'm not saying that it doesn't serve you jolly well right, I still think you're entitled to enjoy some of your holiday while you're here. And I said I wanted revenge,' he reminded her softly, in a way which made her catch her breath until he went on, 'so I decided that, at the very least, you owed it to me to come diving with me after having the audacity to try and get me to teach you to swim.'

And so he had abducted her, knowing that she would love every minute of it! A strange warmth spread through her and she took a deep breath, warning herself to be careful. The sun's heat on her skin was almost erotic—

the quiet lapping of the waves against the boat, too relaxing, and she sat up, hugging her knees.

'You've got some very unorthodox ways of going about things, Aaron Blake.' It was difficult forcing a reproval into her voice when it trembled so much. 'Couldn't you simply have *asked* me this morning?'

Propped up on his elbows, his long, tanned legs, flat abdomen and muscular chest glistened a hard bronze.

'Would you have come?'

Adopting the same position, Romy looked at him levelly, the pose accentuating the high thrust of her breasts.

'No,' she answered, positively. Getting involved with her sister's lover—or ex-lover, as the case may have been—was something she had no intention of doing.

She felt Aaron's gaze move down to linger on her breasts—felt the betraying throb of tension in her loins.

'I didn't think so.' He didn't sound at all perturbed. 'But when you get to know me better, Romy, you'll discover that I always get what I want.'

The sunlight was catching the metal rail, dazzling her eyes without her sun-lenses on so that she couldn't see his expression. But she noted the sensual undertone in his voice and guessed that at that moment he wanted *her*—because she was Tania's twin.

'I wanted to take a beautiful woman underwater with me this morning,' he said smoothly, 'and you were the only one I could think of who I could risk taking down without having to watch over like a child. Where did you learn to swim like that?'

He was impressed—she could tell—and she knew a heart-singing pleasure, though more from the way he had suggested she was beautiful than from any compliment about her swimming. Did he really think so? Even when her hair was wet and she had no make-up on?

'My father taught me,' she answered, her eyes misty from remembering those Saturday mornings as a child when Henry Morgan would take her to the local pool before breakfast, before even her mother and Tania were up. 'I think secretly he would have liked a son and I came closer to fitting the bill than Tania because I was the one who always came home with torn clothes and grazed knees. Sometimes he'd take me on one of his fishing weekends and we'd camp and cook fish over a log fire, and just talk about books and...'

She stopped abruptly, feeling the tell-tale tremor behind her words. She hadn't spoken to anyone about him like this since before his death.

'You were close.' It was a gentle observation and Romy nodded, her hand shielding her eyes, not only from the sun, but from the rich, questing clarity of his. She felt as though her emotions—her thoughts—were on show to that impenetrable regard, and she wasn't sure she liked the feeling. For a moment she watched the progress of a small yacht in the distance, its orange sail moving like a silent fin across the water.

'After Mum died there was only Dad...and Tania,' she said quietly.

'So what about the lovely Tania? Why didn't she ever develop her water-wings?'

Aaron's voice was laced with humour, and something else. Sarcasm, Romy thought, because he was still angry with her twin for encouraging Danny Gower. But he still wants Tania, she reminded herself sharply as self-protection which she felt she sorely needed against that striking, male magnetism. Tania. Not you...

'Tania never liked the water,' she told him casually, wiggling her toes and watching how the sun caught the vivid red varnish. 'She never really lost her fear of it.' And with a small giggle, 'Dad used to say it was because a pipe burst and flooded the whole of downstairs the day she was born.'

Through semi-blurred vision she saw him laugh. It was the first time she'd seen him laugh with genuine humour, she realised, and liked it. It softened his features, made him look younger—more approachable—creasing the lines around his eyes and mouth. A light breeze had

struck up, ruffling his hair, and she thought how dev-
astatingly handsome he was—how wonderfully male.
Every muscle and sinew in his body was that of an animal
in peak condition and she wanted to reach out and stroke
that smooth, velvety skin—touch that mat of damp hair
that curled enticingly against his chest.

'You were born on the same day,' he reminded her,
sitting up. 'So how does that account for your aqua-
skills? How much of a gap is there between you,
anyway?'

He smirked when she told him that she was the
younger by ten minutes.

'So little sister learned to sink or swim...cope with
life's problems whenever they arose, is that it?'

He sounded as if he were mocking her, and she wished
she could see his expression more clearly. She would have
liked to have put her glasses on, but he had said she was
beautiful just now, and she didn't want to do anything
to change his opinion.

'I didn't cope very well three months ago when my
father died,' she uttered, almost in self-reproach, and
wondered why she should be telling Aaron Blake. But
he affected her in such a way that she felt compelled to
pour out her feelings, a thing which didn't usually come
very easily to her. 'I went to pieces. I couldn't write a
thing that made any sense...until now...'

She broke off, suddenly realising how he might in-
terpret that.

'Isn't that understandable?' he said softly, getting up,
his almost naked body beautiful as he stood with his
back to the rail. 'You don't lose someone that close to
you without it having a lengthy and sometimes....permanent effect on your life.'

He was looking beyond her—out to sea—and she
guessed from the taut mask of his features that he was
talking from his own, first-hand experience—from a
depth of private bitterness and emotion at which she
could only guess. Above them a bird shrieked—its cry

plaintive and forlorn—before it flapped away towards the indistinct outline of the coast.

'So... what's brought about this sudden new literary spur?'

Suddenly, he was smiling down at her, his deeper feelings cleverly concealed behind the cool mockery of his eyes.

'I don't know.' Romy laughed nervously, the sight of him standing there with his powerful arms folded, his hair blowing back, making her entertain thoughts which shocked her and, grabbing her glasses, she got to her feet. 'The magic of Fiji, I suppose.'

She could hardly tell him the truth—that it was the way he stimulated her both mentally and physically that had got the adrenalin pumping through her to her pen again. But, of course, he knew.

'Are you trying to convince *me* or yourself, that it's only that?' And his voice was low against the sensual murmur of the water. He had moved away from the rail, and Romy swallowed, held there by the probing intensity of his eyes. 'I'm inclined to think it's something infinitely more basic than that.'

'Then you can think what you like.' Her pulse was racing too fast for her to be civil. She turned to go below. And tripped over a rope—straight into his arms.

'Put your glasses on, you silly girl.'

They were being taken from her and placed adroitly on her nose—the features that were mocking her suddenly coming into perfect detail. His eyes were gleaming gold, looking down at her with an amused indulgence, his nostrils slightly flared above the curve of that cruel mouth.

'Are you self-conscious wearing them?'

'No!' She said it too heatedly because he hadn't let her go, and the feel of his bare chest beneath her fingers—the bronzed warmth of his body so close to hers—was making her senses swim. But he *was* right. She was self-conscious wearing her glasses—but only with him.

'I don't know why,' he smiled, as if she hadn't answered him. 'You have a totally natural beauty, Romy...and a more profound effect on me than any other woman I know.'

Now he was really mocking her, she thought, dropping her gaze, and was suddenly shocked to realise that he was right. Her cheeks flamed from the knowledge of his arousal, and he laughed softly at her obvious embarrassment.

'Proof,' he smiled, drawing her towards him, although when he felt her resistance he didn't persist. But neither did he let her go.

'Isn't it mutual?' he murmured, his fingers moving to the tiny pulse beating furiously in her throat—their touch, cool and sensual against it.

'So?' she acknowledged huskily, unwittingly drawing his eyes to the natural pink fullness of her trembling lips. 'I'm sexually attracted to you...so now you know. But that doesn't mean I intend to do anything about it.'

'Why not?' he queried, his eyes raking over her flushed face with some amusement.

She couldn't tell him that it was because she was afraid of him, of how deeply she knew he could hurt her emotionally, and when she remained silent he said, quietly, 'Is there another lover in your life?'

For her emotions' sake, she would have liked to have said there was, but she couldn't lie to him.

'No,' she said, guilelessly, a thin line between her eyes as she added with a catch in her voice, 'But what about Tania?'

She felt the sudden flexing of Aaron's chest muscles— noticed the way he exhaled deeply before answering.

'My feelings for your sister are totally divorced from the way I feel about you, Romy. I've been fighting an irresistible urge to take you to bed ever since I first kissed you.' He grimaced. 'No, before that, if I'm honest...and it isn't helping my control one little bit to know that I'd only have to touch you to turn you into a wildcat in my arms.'

'No!'

She tried to protest as he reached for her glasses, but he was removing them anyway, setting them aside to pull her against him so that he could feel the warmth of her body. She gasped as every nerve-ending suddenly leaped into life, and she heard Aaron's breathing deepen as he kissed the corner of her mouth.

'It's true, isn't it, my sweet?' His voice was low—dangerously persuasive. 'You want me as badly as I want you.'

She wanted to refute his statement, but the fresh, clean dampness of his hair was touching her cheek as his lips sought the sensitive skin below her earlobe, and she couldn't think straight, a small moan escaping her as his tongue traced a pattern of fire down to the tiny beating hollow at her throat. She tensed, shamed by how willingly her body was responding to his expertise, despite the cold isolation and the self-revulsion she felt in letting him do this to her when he had practically admitted that his only interest in her was physical—totally divorced from the real feeling he had for Tania.

She would have murmured her protest then, but his mouth was covering hers, obliterating all thought, and she could only cling to him, a slave to his will as he eased her down on to the sun-washed boards of the deck.

She let out a deep, throaty sound as his full weight came down upon her and, driven by a primeval need, she caught him to her, her long, painted nails clawing down over the hard muscles of his back, making him groan his desire.

'Oh God, girl . . . you're driving me insane. Open your eyes.'

Reluctantly, she let her lids flutter apart, meeting those strong features above her with some surprise. He was every bit the animal in control, yet he looked strangely vulnerable, his cheeks flushed—taut with passion—his eyes darkened by a hunger which both scared and excited her.

Her pulses throbbed as he unfastened her bikini top and removed it, his gaze going from her own flushed cheeks and her kiss-swollen lips, to the pale gold of her shoulders and the paler cream of her breasts.

'You're beautiful,' he said, hoarsely.

She gave a convulsive shudder as he ran his hand across them, moulding one to his palm, and she shut her eyes tightly, embarrassed because he was watching her every response, her teeth clamping down hard on her lip to stop herself crying out—to keep him from guessing just how much he affected her. She was half aware that he had shifted his position because she could feel the sun's hot rays on her face, and then, as his lips suddenly replaced his hand to draw one burgeoning peak into his mouth, she knew a stab of pleasure so great that her body jerked towards him, her gasp as loud as if she had been stung.

'Easy now...easy.'

He was feathering light kisses over her trembling shoulders and breasts, controlling her fevered response with a practised skill.

And suddenly he was asking deeply, 'How many lovers have you had?'

His unexpected query shook her. Did he think her that promiscuous, then?

His smile, though, seemed oddly smug, making her wonder suddenly if it was her lack of sophistication after Tania's that was amusing him and, pride smarting, somehow she got out tightly, 'Enough.'

Aaron's eyebrow lifted, his fingers so light and sensual against the creamy satin of her breast that she closed her eyes against the pleasurable torment they evoked.

'I'm inclined to think otherwise,' she heard him challenge softly, as if he could tell. 'You respond to me as if I were the first...or very nearly...'

'I don't, I...' What was the point of pretending otherwise? He was too experienced not to recognise the meagre degree of experience in her. And though she wanted to convince him that she had had *one* lover—that she wasn't *that* naïve—she couldn't, because his lips were pressing tantalising little kisses against her throat, flooding her veins with desire. And anyway, those early introductions to sex had been clumsy and unfulfilling, and with an inconsiderate lover—never like this!

From somewhere, a high whining sound tried to drag her back to reason, but his mouth was covering hers with such raw ecstasy that she was lost to everything but the scent and sound and feel of Aaron—of his hands and the urgent message they conveyed for total possession of her body.

Then the whining grew louder—a deafening sound coming straight towards them. And suddenly the boat seemed to rock. She heard Aaron's sharp gasp, felt his body jerk convulsively, pinning her painfully against the hard deck as the water swept over them. Then, raucous laughter as the other boat sped away, having ascertained that they were both thoroughly drenched.

'I'm sorry.' Aaron raised himself up on his elbows—cast a disparaging glance over his shoulder. 'A few boisterous teenagers enjoying a prank.' His eyes were dark with concern, and there were rivulets running down his chest into that mat of coarse hair. 'Did I hurt you?'

She was breathing raggedly beneath him, her hair a soft, dishevelled cloud as she shook her head. All she could feel now was shame that she had almost let him make love to her, and hot colour deepened the sensual flush on her skin. If it hadn't been for that other boat deliberately coming too close...

'Don't you think it's time we got back?' she suggested bitingly, not wanting to admit, even to herself, how near she had been to offering him total surrender. 'You've obviously satisfied your warped sense of revenge by dragging me out of bed this morning... and if it's all the same to you, I *did* come here to work.'

She was being childish and ungrateful, but she couldn't help herself, driven by a rising fear that, despite all her intentions to the contrary, she was becoming dangerously involved with him—emotionally as well as phys-

ically. Which was totally insane, she warned herself,
because when the month was up and she left here, the
chances were she would never see him again.

She felt the first stab of some cutting emotion, intensifying when she saw the way his mouth twisted cruelly—
how his features darkened against the hard blue of the
sky.

'Sorry, I forgot,' he said, in a voice tight with anger.
'My kisses are only acceptable to you if you're trying to
fool me...or if we've got an audience. Then it's all right,
isn't it?'

And he stormed away from her to restart the engine.
Which was probably just as well, she thought, chastened, because she wouldn't have known how to answer
him. And, miserably, she had to endure a cool silence
from him for the whole of the journey home.

Aaron's coolness towards her continued over the following days, yet in spite of it Romy found herself stimulated by his company. He shared her love of books, for
one thing, even lending her several from his own library,
all of which she read and returned one by one, and en-
joyed discussing with him at length over some quiet
lunch, during a walk, or over dinner. He knew a lot about
both the classics and modern literature. In fact, for his
age, he knew a lot about life in general, Romy discovered, and it was this vast knowledge of his—his
overall intellect—that scared her just a little, made her
aware of an increasing admiration and respect for him—
and something else, too, which she didn't even want to
think about.

He organised new contact lenses for her and, despite
her protests, insisted on bearing the cost of them himself.
'Since,' he remarked, drily, 'it was on my property that
your others came to grief.' And in return, Romy kept
her part of the bargain and, as Tania, accompanied him
wherever he saw fit to take her.

But that cool courtesy of his was wearing down her
resistance to him—making her more and more aware of

that dangerous sexual chemistry between them which was lying just below the surface, threatening to flare like some uncontrolled fire whenever she was with him. And he saw to it that she was—often.

Intent on being seen with her—for whatever motives—he took her to expensive restaurants, to the parties to which they were jointly invited, but which, to Romy's relief, he always seemed keen to leave after only a couple of hours; and sometimes he took her to a *meke* in one of the villages—a colourful story depicted by a programme of traditional dance and song—while Romy watched with delight, noting the costumes made from printed bark cloth, flowers and leaves, and the music which was provided by the *lali*—a drum carved from the bark of a tree—and a hollow bamboo pole beaten rhythmically on the ground. But Aaron arranged it that they were never entirely alone, nor had he attempted to kiss her again since that day on his boat and, despite this almost overwhelming attraction to him, Romy knew she should have been glad.

He was in love with Tania, she kept goading herself. And even if she could forget that—convince herself also that she wouldn't be hurting Tania if she did take the pleasure her body craved from his in an affair with him, since her twin preferred Danny—how could she face the sort of pain she knew she would have to suffer when eventually she had to leave him and go home? When she also knew that he would so easily let her? She couldn't.

Nevertheless, feigned immunity didn't stop her heart missing a beat when he took her in his arms on the dance floor, or her breath catching in her chest as he pulled out a chair for her in a restaurant on one occasion and his hand accidentally brushed hers. He had been aware of how she'd flinched at that casual contact—obvious from the quizzical look he'd given her—but he hadn't made any comment, simply sitting down himself and ordering lunch in that deep, resonant voice which made waiters subservient and Romy's nerve-endings throb.

She was in love with him. In that small, intimate restaurant that day she finally admitted it to herself. Why else would she take so much pleasure from his smile? The odd compliment he gave her? Or a glance from those beautiful amber eyes—however brief? And if he'd wanted everyone else to think that they were lovers, then he had succeeded—but with a cost to her heart, she thought, ironically—because she hadn't been bothered by that awful Danny Gower since. Just being seen with Aaron Blake was enough, it seemed, to brand her his. Even Sandra Donnington was fooled.

'Are you two anywhere near as serious as rumour has it?'

The four of them were drinking cocktails on the terrace—Theo included—and Sandra's frank question was directed at Aaron.

Breath held, Romy couldn't look at him, wondering what he would say, as aware of him as of the warm evening breeze which came off the ocean and caressed her bare shoulders.

'Are we...Tania?'

The directness of his question shook her and she looked up, meeting his eyes with a hard accusation in her own. How dared he ask that when he was only using her for his own ends?

She fought against a sudden surge of anger and pain, a wry twist to her glossy red lips. 'If one listens to rumour...one invariably gets the facts wrong,' she uttered dispassionately, but she could feel her heart hammering against her breastbone, the colour creeping up her throat.

Aaron's mouth tightened, his eyes darkening, and Romy turned away, finding that hard gaze unsettling. So let him be angry, she thought, if I've just destroyed the image he's been so intent on creating.

'Pity,' Sandra laughed, sipping a delicious-looking Singapore Sling. 'Aaron needs a woman to look after him,' she outlined in that half-sisterly, half-maternal way of hers, 'though he's too proud to admit as much, aren't you dear?' Fondly, she slipped her arm through his, her smile challenging him to deny it, and Romy felt that inevitable little twist of envy at the obvious affection between them.

'Perhaps...like my beautiful young guest...I'm simply not prepared to commit myself.' Aaron sounded amused, but Romy detected something dark and mysterious flickering in his eyes, something she couldn't quite define.

Disconcerted, she shifted her gaze, ostensibly to watch Theo take the cellophane from his cigar, and she felt even more uncomfortable when she noticed how intently the older man was studying her, a hint of a smile curving the hard mouth.

'No,' he said suddenly, drawing the cigar across the grey moustache to inhale its aroma. 'She doesn't commit herself to very much at all, does she?'

Romy tensed, giving him a half-wary smile. He could only be referring to the way she often evaded his questions about her supposed television career, and she caught her breath as she heard his casual, 'I think there's a lot more to the beautiful Tania than meets the eye.'

He couldn't have made a truer statement! Swallowing—dreading being found out—Romy shot a glance at Aaron, silently enlisting his help.

His mouth pulled down one side, and his eyes didn't leave hers as he drawled in response, 'Believe me, Theo...there is.'

Romy stiffened, glaring at him. He was enjoying this! she realised in annoyance, her attention suddenly caught by Theo putting a flame to his cigar with an expensive, gold lighter.

'A habit I've been telling him to break for years.'

Turning, Romy noticed Aaron's gaze, fixed, as hers had been, on the rising cloud of blue smoke.

'It's bad for his health.'

Picking up his glass, Theo gave a snort of disapproval. 'And only Aaron, my dear,' he commented to Romy, 'would dare to question *anything* I do.'

'Only because he cares about you, Theo,' Sandra was quick to defend, laughingly. 'And because he's probably the only person who isn't afraid to let you know what he thinks.'

Romy smiled, one swift glance taking in both men. Sandra was probably right, she thought. In terms of tenacity—strength of will—there didn't seem to be much to choose between them.

And she realised then how cleverly Aaron had changed the subject, drawing the conversation away from *her* with an amazing subtlety, and again she couldn't look at him, feeling the dark intensity of that gaze.

A maid had come out to announce dinner and the four of them rose, with Sandra and Theo first to go inside. Relieved, Romy made to do the same, and was stalled by Aaron's hand on her arm, his touch light, but firm enough to keep her there.

'Relax,' he advised, softly, 'you're too tense. Anyway, Theo's going home tomorrow.' His eyes took in the little pulse beating in the hollow of her throat before travelling down over the pale gold of her shoulders and the folds of soft chiffon which were stirring in the light wind, and a half-amused, half-sensual smile touched his lips.

'To think that if that little wood-carving you bought hadn't started me thinking that there must be two of you, I might still have been taking things at face value like everyone else.'

So that was what had finally betrayed her to him! she thought hectically, remembering how interestedly he had been studying it when he'd picked it up that day. But her heart had started beating too fast because he was drawing her close, and in panic she caught the stimulating scent of his aftershave lotion—felt the disturbing proximity of his body.

He merely laughed softly at the rebellious glitter in her eyes.

'I like knowing something about you that no one else does,' he breathed, his gaze running over the provocatively accentuated eyes and lips—the slim column of her throat. 'It makes me feel . . . privileged.'

A sensual little tremor ran through her as his other arm went around her middle, and it took all her mental strength not to let him see what he was doing to her.

'Don't you mean powerful?' she snapped back, wishing his cologne wasn't making her feel quite so heady. 'After all, you only have to threaten me with telling Theo I'm not Tania, and you know I'll do anything you ask.'

'*Anything* I ask?'

He laughed again and that dark, compelling magnetism met a tug of desire in her which she didn't want to recognise. It wasn't yet dark, so the terrace lights still hadn't been switched on, and behind them the bougainvillaea turned to fire in the sunset, in startling contrast to the white walls of the house.

'Oh, would that were true, my beautiful Romy....although I don't think you're as opposed to my methods as you're pretending to be.'

She looked at him pointedly, pushing back a strand of hair. 'And what's that supposed to mean?'

A bird dived out of the cypress tree near the steps, startling her with its agitated shriek of alarm.

'I mean that you want to be in my arms as much as I want you here, and by my taking the choice away from you, you can ease your conscience about enjoying the intimacy by convincing yourself it's been entirely forced upon you. Isn't that the truth?'

'No!' Oh God, he knew her too well! 'Let me go!'

'Then why are you trembling?' Ignoring her request, he pulled her closer, his strength ridiculing her vain attempts to be free. 'Cold? Or is it repressed passion that you'd rather die than admit to?'

His body was strong and warm and arousing—too arousing, Romy realised frantically. Desperate that he shouldn't guess the truth—have the satisfaction of knowing that he was right—she pushed against him, finding the hard wall of his chest unyielding beneath the dark, silk shirt.

'Let me go!'

This time his hold relaxed, although he still kept her within the circle of his arms.

'What are you afraid of, Romy?' he asked quietly, and his voice was so gentle—his eyes flickering with such dark concern—that it took an immense strength of will not to tell him.

You. And myself, because I'm in love with you!

Shuddering, she wondered how he would have reacted if she *had* said that. Simply been amused, probably.

So she spat back, in defiance of her thumping heart, 'Nothing. Nothing that my leaving here wouldn't put right!' And noticed the hard gleam in his eyes—the tightening of his lips—as she tugged free at last and swept past him into the house.

Theo had asked her if she would drive him to the airport the next day since his cousin wasn't going to be able to, suggesting that she take him in the estate car which he had been using since his arrival.

'It will save Aaron, or someone else, having to pick it up later,' he had advised her, and so Romy had found herself unable to refuse.

Nevertheless, the mid-morning journey had her on edge for most of the way, dreading that Theo would ask awkward questions she couldn't easily answer, but she need not have worried. He seemed quiet—in a pensive mood today.

Still she would be more than relieved when he was safely on his plane, she couldn't help thinking shamefully, and started as he suddenly spoke to her.

'We didn't come to any conclusions yesterday, Tania.' He was looking her way, tugging at the ends of the silky moustache. 'Are you and Aaron serious about each other?'

The sun caught the silver highlights as she turned, glancing at Theo with guarded eyes, not sure what to say. After all, she didn't know what Aaron's intentions were towards her twin, or even how Tania felt about him, and she experienced a dull ache around her heart.

'Would you disapprove?' she asked, quietly.

Out of the corner of her eye she noticed the man studying her discomfitingly.

'I'd like to see him settle down,' he said, his voice as expressionless as his features. Where concealing emotions was concerned, both men were experts at it, Romy realised.

They were passing fields of sugar cane, and she glanced out at the native men in their loose-fitting clothes and white hats cutting the ripe crop, while others packed it on to trucks.

'It's been a good year.'

Her moment's distraction hadn't escaped that keen perception—again a trait both men possessed.

'Yes, I know,' Romy answered, wondering who had told her that, and remembered that it was that awful Danny Gower, the day he'd driven her home.

'My cousin needs a woman with brains...and you've got them,' Theo surprised her, both with his compliment and his frankness. 'He needs a wife...children of his own. I know he can be very cynical towards the opposite sex...towards marriage as a whole...but I was hoping you might be able to change all that, Tania.'

There was an uncharacteristic softening in the hazel eyes—so at variance with the hard-boned structure of his face—and guilt flowed with the misery inside of her.

She couldn't tell him that there was no more chance of Aaron marrying *her* than there was of there being life on Mars, and she was glad when they had reached the airport—when they were inside the building, saying their farewells.

She didn't think she could have kept up this pretence another minute, she thought, watching his tall figure striding away. And suddenly she froze, aghast.

Theo had stopped dead and, like her, was having difficulty believing what his eyes were telling him as he looked back at her and then at the other girl who had just come through Customs.

Tania!

CHAPTER SEVEN

DROPPING a suitcase, Tania was running forward to hug her twin.

'Rom——' she started to say enthusiastically, but Romy cut in quickly.

'Romy! Fancy seeing you here!' Her heart was pounding, every nerve alert. 'I was just seeing Theo off. Theo Stanley...my *landlord*,' she emphasised in warning as the man came up to them.

'Your *landlord*?' Tania looked puzzled. Then, recovering quickly, she offered him a brilliant smile and a beautifully manicured hand. 'I'm Romy,' she introduced herself, quick to catch on. 'Tania's identical twin sister.'

And more identical they had never been, Romy thought, feeling as though she were looking at a reflection of herself as Tania pulled off a blue and white spotted head scarf, shaking free the highlighted blonde bob. And when she removed her sunglasses, revealing the identical, almond-shaped blue eyes, Romy noticed that even the colour of their eye shadow was the same dusky blue.

'Good God! There are two of you!'

Theo's total bemusement brought a burst of high-pitched laughter from Tania, but Romy's stomach turned over. She couldn't bear the thought of Theo finding out that she had been deceiving him—not at this late stage. Apart from anything else, she had grown to like him, even if she did still find him intimidating at times.

'Everyone reacts in the same way,' she smiled, avoiding his eyes by taking one of Tania's cases from her. And, thinking quickly, 'Romy hopes to finish her book while she's here. She writes, you see.'

Which was hardly a lie, was it? she consoled her conscience above the hubbub of a busy airport.

Theo was shaking his head as he looked repeatedly from one girl to the other.

'There isn't a scrap of difference between you.' He tugged thoughtfully at his moustache. 'No doubt you've had some fun in your time confusing people.'

Tania's eyes crinkled mischievously as she caught Romy's arm.

'Haven't we just, sis?' she tittered, without the slightest hint of guilt, though Romy felt her cheeks reddening.

Somehow she managed to smile. 'Look . . . we mustn't let Theo miss his plane, must we, Tania?' she uttered through gritted teeth, and was relieved when the announcement for the departure of the Lautoka flight came over the intercom.

Theo glanced over his shoulder at the sudden activity as everyone started moving towards the departure bay, turning back to say frowningly, 'Does Aaron know about this?'

Romy smiled again awkwardly, wishing he would go. 'Of course.' And beside her, felt the sharp glance her sister put her way. Naturally, she thought Aaron was still away, Romy realised. Well, did she have a few things to say to Tania!

'What was he doing here?' her twin was asking as soon as Theo disappeared into the crowd. 'And what did he mean about Aaron knowing? Aaron's away.' Blue eyes met Romy's cautiously. 'Isn't he?'

Romy took a deep breath, biting back words of annoyance from the pent-up tensions inside of her.

'No, he isn't,' she succeeded in saying calmly as they walked out into the sunlit car park. 'And you and I are going to have a little chat about that.'

Tania gave a tight, high-pitched laugh and replaced her sunglasses. 'Oh God! Does he know?'

Behind her own dark lenses, Romy's eyes narrowed as she noted the amusement in her twin's voice. 'What do *you* think?' she asked, scathingly.

Tania clearly didn't need to. 'Oh, poor Romy!' It was an attempt at sympathy, though she was biting her glossy, lower lip to prevent the grin she was having difficulty concealing. 'He must have put you through hell!'

'Right first time.' Romy's voice was clipped as she took the car keys out of her handbag. 'You might have warned me that he was your lover,' she rebuked, the words catching in her throat.

'Did he...' Tania broke off abruptly, causing Romy to turn. Her sister had stopped dead, beautiful in a simple, cotton suit. The same blue as her own dress, she noted absently, remembering how they often turned up in the same colour, much to the other's surprise. 'What's gone on exactly between you two?' Tania wanted to know, her smooth brow furrowing.

'Nothing, I assure you,' Romy attempted lightly, shame over what had almost happened between her and her sister's boyfriend bringing a flush to her cheeks. 'He's still all yours, sister dear, and you're welcome to him.' Well, she had to say something to hide her true feelings— the pain she was suddenly experiencing with the realisation that now her twin was back, Aaron would probably have no further interest in her.

'Getting pretty thick with him though, aren't we... borrowing his car?'

Unlocking the estate vehicle, Romy couldn't miss the hint of possessiveness behind Tania's remark. Which could only mean that her twin still cared about him, Romy decided, her heart seeming to give a little twist.

Helping to put her sister's suitcases into the back of the car, she took great pains to explain how she had only borrowed it to bring Theo here.

'I tried to telephone you as soon as I discovered Aaron was here,' she said defensively, starting the ignition as Tania slid in beside her, 'but you'd already left. What are you doing here, anyway?' It was only then that she remembered to ask, disconcerted as she had been during those few tense moments inside. Frowningly, she continued, 'I thought you were on the safari job...'

Tania fingered the immaculately groomed hair, a heavy French perfume cloying in the confines of the car.

'Malcolm...our producer...went down with...oh, swamp fever or something, so the whole thing's been cancelled, and I can't say I'm sorry. It must have been two hundred degrees in the shade!'

It was familiar and expected—this exaggeration of Tania's. But, feeling as desolate as she did at that moment, Romy found it particularly irritating.

'Can't you ever say exactly what you mean? State facts as they are?' she said rather impatiently, going to change gear and then remembering that the car was automatic. 'No one here was supposed to know you *that* well, were they?' Indignantly, she turned to meet the identical features across the small space. 'So I come here expecting a few weeks' peace and solitude and what do I find? That one of your wronged menfriends—namely Aaron Blake—is not only here when he isn't supposed to be, but is taking out his pent-up frustrations on me, thinking I'm you. That people are ringing me asking me to parties. That I'm being pursued by a rather insipid and very determined reporter...and that you've been having an affair with a married man!'

Steering the large car around a bend, Romy heard her sister's sharp, indrawn breath. 'Oh hell! Quintin Swain. Has he been snooping around again?' And when Romy, carefully overtaking a lorry, explained about her first and subsequent meetings with him, Tania responded with, 'Oh, I see.' Adding, 'I dated him once...ages ago. But one evening with him was just about all I could stand. The brush-off was too much of a blow to his ego and he's been bent on getting even with me ever since.'

'Great!' Romy tossed a glance skywards as she brought the car safely into the nearside lane again, and out of the corner of her eye saw Tania's hand run over a sheer-stockinged leg.

'I'm sorry, sis...I didn't mean to get you into a mess,' she said, suddenly more serious—contrite. 'It was just unfortunate that you had to bump into Quintin on that plane. If he hadn't seen you . . . and with the house being as isolated as it is . . . no one would have found out you were here,' she added, sympathetically, 'because it's only Sandra Donnington and one or two others who know me really well.'

And Quintin had told Sandra, Romy remembered on reflection.

'Oh, and Aaron, of course,' Tania was saying, 'and I didn't dream for one moment *he'd* be here, I swear. I know I'm rather scatter-brained at times...perhaps even thoughtless,' she admitted with a self-deprecating grimace, 'but I'd never have subjected my own sister to a hard, shrewd animal like that.' Her obvious concern sent a sudden surge of affection through Romy as her twin went on, 'You know, I had vibes that everything wasn't right, but I thought it was my over-active imagination.' She pulled a wry face. 'Obviously I was wrong.'

And obviously that bond of communication was still there between them, Romy realised heart-warmingly, even if Tania had misunderstood those waves of desperation.

'Oh, and by the way, I'd like *you* to know, even if no one else believes me,' Tania expressed, 'I wasn't having an affair with Danny. It is Danny Gower we're talking about, isn't it?'

Romy shot her a sceptical look, blue eyes wide. 'You mean there could be others?'

'Of course not.' Casually, Tania glanced out of the window at the numerous bazaars and market stalls they were passing, which boasted baskets and shells and the best of the island's handicrafts. 'Married men never were my forte.' A slim shoulder lifted beneath the blue cotton jacket. 'It was only a harmless flirtation, anyway.'

'A harmless flirtation!' Pulling away from a junction, Romy looked at her sister, aghast. 'Tania, he's not only got a wife . . . he's got a seven-year-old daughter as well.'

Her throat contracted as she thought how easily the child's security could be destroyed—just as Aaron's had been all those years ago.

'Has he?' There was a note of weary uninterest in Tania's voice. 'Well, he can keep them,' she was commenting, her red lips twisting wryly. 'I only made use of his attentions last time to make Aaron jealous.'

'Why?' Romy glanced disbelievingly at her. 'Are you...in love with him?' she ventured, breath held.

'Oh, Romy, come on! What girl wouldn't be?' Tania gave a careless wave of her hand. 'And you can't tell me he hasn't got through to the woman behind that studious exterior of yours because you'd be fibbing if you did. He's as sexy as hell!'

She didn't need her sister to tell her that, any more than she needed that curious blue gaze on her flushed cheeks, and she made a pointless exercise of adjusting an already perfectly aligned rear-view mirror as a distraction from her emotions—the hopelessness she was suddenly feeling.

'Anyway, when you're as experienced as I am, love, you'll find that there are some men you can't bring to their knees just by playing it cool...you know....withholding favours.' To Romy's relief, Tania wasn't pursuing the subject of her twin's feelings. 'And Aaron Blake's one of them. So I thought I'd turn Danny's interest in me to my own ends, to show Aaron that I wouldn't wait around for ever...to get him to commit himself more. Instead, he went wild.' There was rebellion in the full, glossy lips. 'In front of Niki, too.'

After negotiating another bend, Romy looked at her sister. 'Do you know why?' she asked softly, understanding, such a surge of love for Aaron welling up inside her that it hurt.

'Yes...because he's so damn moral,' Tania bit out, making Romy wince at the thought of how unthinkingly her sister seemed to be behaving. But, surprisingly, she suspected that Tania didn't know the facts about Aaron's childhood, and right at that moment she didn't feel like enlightening her. Right then she wanted to be in his arms. To feel his lips—his hands—moving intimately over her body as they had that morning on his boat. But cruel reason was surfacing, forcing her to remember that it was Tania he would want as soon as he knew she was back, and from what her twin had said, she still wanted him, too. And it wasn't as if she, Romy, had tried to delude herself that it had been any more than desire in his eyes whenever he'd looked at her—kissed *her*. So why did it hurt so much to accept that now?

'I thought you'd be pleased to see me,' Romy heard her sister remark, as she stared through the windscreen, trying to blink away the sudden mist in front of her eyes. 'Instead you look as miserable as if you've just had your latest book rejected.'

Romy inhaled deeply, glad that she was wearing dark glasses so that Tania couldn't see her tears.

'I'm sorry,' she apologised, managing a smile. 'Of course I'm glad to see you. Not to mention relieved! It's all been rather a strain...pretending to be you.'

They were leaving the busy streets and crowded bazaars behind them, the hills and quiet grasslands stretching away in front of them.

'I thought you said Aaron knew.' Tania sounded puzzled. 'Surely you dropped the pretence...' Her words tailed off, her expression puzzling, and Romy explained.

'Theo was here.' She pressed her foot harder to the floor to take the open stretch of road. 'It's Theo who owns the house, remember? And Aaron said he wouldn't tell him...' She broke off, disinclined to divulge to her sister the conditions Aaron had laid down in return for his silence. After all, she had her pride. And Tania would be bound to find out soon enough, if not from her, then from Aaron.

'Not any more he doesn't.'

Romy looked across at her sister, so engrossed in her own thoughts that she had lost the train of the conversation. 'Doesn't what?' she asked, baffled.

'Own the house.' Tania looked equally as puzzled. 'Didn't he mention it to you...thinking you were me?'

Romy shook her head, her eyebrows drawn together. 'No.'

'How odd,' said Tania absently, taking an envelope out of her bag. 'The sale went through during the past couple of weeks apparently, and this new Tenancy Agreement was waiting for me when I got back to the flat on Thursday. And guess who owns the house now? Aaron Blake!'

The car shuddered violently as Romy's foot jerked against the accelerator.

'You mean, he owns your house?' she exhaled, her mind swimming, colour surging into her cheeks.

'Yes . . . what's wrong?'

Tania was looking at her curiously, probably wondering why her sister looked so murderous, but Romy couldn't tell her, such hot anger pumping through her that she wasn't fully in control of the car.

He had used her—totally and unscrupulously. That was all her brain could digest. Virtually blackmailed her into acting as Tania by using the house as a weapon against her, when all the time he was buying the place himself! So it wouldn't have mattered if he had told his cousin, she realised now, seething, because there was only one person who had had the power to terminate Tania's tenancy, and it had been him all along!

But why hadn't Theo mentioned it at some stage? she asked herself numbly, her knuckles showing white where they gripped the wheel. Like the night she had first met him when he'd been questioning her about the house? Or at the airport earlier when she'd introduced him as her landlord? Had Aaron asked him not to say anything? And if so, why? Because he'd have had no power to wield against her? Because he'd known that she could refuse to do what he wanted of her—drop the pretence with no threat at all to Tania's tenancy—if she'd known that the house no longer belonged to Theo? And he'd hardly have been able to convince *her* that he would do anything himself to stop Tania coming here when he obviously still wanted her twin. But just how much Romy had only just come to realise.

Tears blurred her vision and she was shaking so much—so awash with humiliation and hurt anger—she didn't see the other car coming until it was too late.

She heard Tania's frantic, 'Look out!', the other driver's horn blaring, and she was spinning the wheel furiously, hearing a deafening screech of tyres as she hit the brake hard. But the car was out of control. She felt the violent impact as the nearside wing caught a tree. Heard the sickening crunch of metal. And it took several moments of desperately trying to regain control before she realised that the other car had gone past without even bothering to stop, and that they themselves had miraculously ended up the right way up, half-way down a grassy bank.

She looked anxiously at Tania. Her face was deathly pale and her eyes were closed.

'Tania?' she whispered, shaking her gently by the arm, hardly daring to breathe. Then, more frantically, 'Tania, speak to me!'

For one half-crazed moment she thought her sister was dead, until Tania's eyes flickered open and she murmured, 'What am I supposed to say?'

Romy let out a deep sigh, her smile relieved. Even in a situation like this her sister could still be flippant.

'Are you all right?'

Tania nodded, casting a glance over her slender limbs as if to make doubly certain.

'You?'

Romy grimaced, then winced as she gripped her right arm. There was some slight bruising from where she had been thrown against the door, but apart from that she seemed remarkably unscathed. In fact, they had both been very lucky. Thank goodness they had been wearing seat-belts!

Shakily, she opened her door and clambered out to inspect the damage to the car. Dismayed, she saw that not only was the front bumper hanging off, but that there was a large dent in the wing, and the nearside headlamp was smashed.

'Oh no!' she groaned, wretchedly.

Near to tears, she felt Tania's arm around her. 'It wasn't your fault, love,' she heard her sister say soothingly, her perfume—the familiar scent of her—comforting now. 'It was that idiot's for being on the wrong side of the road . . . and he couldn't even bother to stop.'

Romy groaned again, rubbing her bruised arm. 'Try explaining that to Aaron.'

'Ooh-ooh!' Tania grimaced. 'I'd forgotten about him. Never mind, Romy . . . things could have been worse. He could have lent you the Ferrari!'

'Oh, Tania . . . don't.' To her own surprise she suddenly burst into tears, and she felt the reassurance of her sister's warm cheek, soft against her own. Tania had always acted as big sister, Romy remembered fondly, during their childhood, as adolescents, and since. And in spite of her butterfly life-style, her twin had given her immense comfort when their father had died, Romy recalled affectionately. And before—long before that—after that first bitter romance . . .

And now, for a few weak moments, she was glad to let her sister slip into that old role.

'He's really got you wound up, hasn't he?' said Tania gently, half curiously. 'What were you so angry about, anyway, when I told you he'd bought the house?'

She still didn't feel up to explaining to Tania. Nor could she tell her that it wasn't so much what Aaron was going to say that had started her blubbering like a child—even if he was likely to think her a careless woman driver, and probably, typically, in his opinion. What she was really upset about was that she loved him with every feminine cell in her body, and when Tania had walked through that airport, guiltily Romy had wished she hadn't, because she'd lost all hope of ever making him love *her*.

'Let's thumb a lift to the nearest telephone,' she said, getting a grip on herself and sniffing back her tears.

'Then we can ring a garage to come and tow in the car...and get ourselves a cab home.'

Tania looked dubious, raking long fingernails through the highlightened hair.

'Shouldn't we just ring Aaron and tell him what happened? I mean, he'll be much more adept at dealing with a situation like this...'

'No,' Romy cut in, determinedly. 'I put the thing off the road and I'm going to be responsible for getting it back on. Anyway, he isn't home today. He had business inland, so with a bit of luck we might be able to get a repair job started before he even finds out.'

'You aren't suggesting that we don't even tell...'

'Aren't I?' Romy stated positively, to her astounded twin. 'The last thing I feel like right now is being hauled over the coals by Aaron Blake, so unless you've got a better idea, let's get our thumbs busy.'

The exercise proved successful. Within a couple of hours they had arranged for the car's safe delivery to a garage and managed, after great difficulty, to book a panel-beating job and respray for the following day, though only after they had decided it would help to tell the native proprietor that the car belonged to Aaron Blake. The mere mention of his name could work miracles, Romy found, although she left strict instructions that the vehicle and the bill for repairs should be delivered personally to her as soon as the work had been carried out. After all, Aaron had suggested that morning that she borrow the car for her own private use—although she had refused his offer, not wanting to feel indebted to him in any way—so he probably wouldn't think it odd if she didn't take the car back for a day or two. He'd probably just assume she'd changed her mind, she thought, hopefully.

She felt decidedly better about the whole incident, although the strain of the day had brought on a headache, so that when her sister suggested going out that evening, Romy declined.

'I think I'll just take a good book to bed,' she smiled, glad that she could at least be herself now when she did go out. She had suffered worse bruising, though, than she had at first realised, and her whole body ached—craved the soothing luxury of a warm bath.

'Well, perhaps it's for the best,' Tania accepted, her face concerned as she eyed her sister who was curled up in a chair. 'You do look a bit peaky. Would you promise me one thing, though?'

Romy looked up suspiciously. 'No more hare-brained schemes,' she warned half chidingly, and Tania laughed.

'No, silly. All I'm asking is that if you see Aaron to-night, don't mention yet that I'm back. I need to build up some reserves of ammunition before I face that man's temper, and something tells me he's going to be more than a little bit angry with me for sending you in my place...especially after the way I walked out on him last time. Tomorrow will be soon enough...and let's hope that when he sees me the element of surprise will serve as my best defence against that wonderfully wild streak of his.'

She gave a deep, sensual shudder as she paced the lounge in a red bra and slip, filing a varnished nail, and from the depths of the wicker chair, Romy studied her twin wonderingly. It wasn't like Tania to worry about what any man said or thought, but, of course, this one was special. And perhaps in Aaron she had finally met her match...

Pain cut into her as she imagined the two of them together—two beautiful people making love, their limbs entwined, their bodies blending, their passionate natures perfectly suited. It could only take a man like Aaron to bring Tania under control, she thought, reaching for her knitting in the basket beside the chair as a diversion from the anguish which stabbed her chest, making breathing difficult. It had been two weeks since she had touched it, she realised now, her writing having been too prolific for her to need anything else.

'Why did you? Walk out on him, I mean?' she asked
Tania as casually as she could manage. 'When he thought
I was you he asked me if it was to avoid adverse pub-
licity... because of Danny Gower.'

Tania gave another little laugh, high-pitched—re-
soundingly feminine.

'Of course not...I hadn't done anything wrong. I
simply wanted to teach him a lesson for shouting at me
in front of one of the servants. Obviously, he couldn't
take a woman doing that to him. I should imagine it's
always been the other way around...so I suppose he
preferred to think I left because I was scared of the Press.
But you know what I've always said...even bad publicity is still publicity. It gets you noticed.'

Romy couldn't wholly agree with that. One would have
to be pretty thick-skinned, she thought, not to be affected by ill criticism, particularly if it were made public.
Still, she had no fears about seeing Aaron tonight.

'Don't worry...as soon as you've gone I'm having a
bath and going straight to bed,' she informed Tania positively, 'so your secret's quite safe with me.'

'Thanks,' Tania threw over her shoulder as she went
into the bedroom, emerging minutes later, looking rav-
ishing with a red velvet jacket slung over a slinky, black
dress.

'I might be late...so don't lie awake,' she advised
almost maternally, giving Romy a light peck on the cheek
as her cab arrived.

'I won't,' Romy promised, although she felt uneasy
about her sister going out alone, even on this beautiful
island paradise. But then, she reminded herself, Tania
never had been one to stay in for a whole evening—even
as a teenager—which was why she had found her own
flat as soon as she was old enough, because of Henry
Morgan's increasing disapproval of the hours and the
company she kept. Not that either had retarded her career
in any way, Romy thought warmly, pouring herbal-
scented crystals into a steamy, running bath. Her twin
might be somewhat of a rebel, but she was one of those

people who attracted good fortune like a magnet attracts steel—which brought her thoughts round to Aaron.

Removing her clothes and stepping into the foaming water, she felt an ache the crystals couldn't soothe away at the thought of how he had used her. The accident had forced Tania's revelation about this house to the back of her mind, but now it returned viciously, gnawing at her, producing first anger, then humiliation, then anger again.

Why had he done it? The question still burned through her as she was towelling herself dry. Why had he deceived her—forced her into a position where she had had to comply with his demands? Did he despise her so much for misleading him in the beginning that he wanted to punish her in some way? And at the same time satisfy his masculine ego by proving, by dint of his sexual expertise, that she wasn't immune to that dynamic and powerful sexuality of his? After all, she wasn't, she reflected, slipping into a flimsy, pink wrap—and he knew that, as surely as she did herself. Just thinking of the way he could arouse her sent a kick of desire through her loins—made her breasts ache in futile response. Or perhaps, she thought, with her breath catching in her chest, he really had been so sick with jealousy over Tania that he'd been prepared to do anything to make everyone believe she was still his, which would be a far more logical explanation as to why he had exploited her so unscrupulously.

She forced back a sob in her throat as someone knocked at the front door.

Aaron! It had to be, she thought, panicking, and was still trying to compose herself when her worst fears were confirmed.

'Romy?' He was casually dressed—looking hot and dishevelled —and, without her glasses she wasn't sure, but she thought she saw relief in his face.

'I—I wasn't expecting you,' she faltered, wondering if, in the darkness, he'd noticed the absence of the car.

'No?' He took time to enjoy a long, leisurely study of her body beneath the clinging wrap, before stepping inside. 'From the look of you I would have thought otherwise.'

She blushed profusely, telling herself that it was useless trying not to let this very disturbing man in dark shirt and trousers affect her. Her pulse was already beating at twice its normal pace.

'Do you want some coffee?' She turned towards the kitchen and felt his hand on her arm, stalling her.

'No.'

She glanced back at him, too aware of the warmth of his hand through her soft, satin sleeve, and her throat constricted.

'What then?'

His gaze raked over her, the firm mouth moving at the corners. 'Haven't you got something to tell me?'

In her bare feet he seemed to tower over her, his gaping shirt exposing a chest too disconcertingly male, and Romy swallowed, feeling the pull of his magnetism sparking off treacherous responses in her body. Surely he couldn't know about the car? Or was it Tania's arrival he had somehow found out about?

'Like what?' she queried, lifting her small chin to meet the hard amber of his eyes.

A black eyebrow lifted reprovingly. 'Like the little accident you had on the way back from the airport this afternoon.'

There was a moment's tense silence during which she thought she might very well be sick.

'Oh, that!' She tried to feign a careless, Tania-like laugh which didn't quite come off. 'It was only a little scratch...really.'

There was an almost feral gleam in his eyes as they scanned her strained features, making her cast her tongue over her lips.

'A virtually severed front bumper and a nearside panel needing beating out and respraying? Oh, and a new nearside headlamp.' His cynicism was evident. 'I'd hate to know your idea of real damage.'

'It wasn't my fault,' she said defensively. 'If the other car had been on the right side of the road we...'

'We?' he prompted, frowning, when she stopped abruptly. 'Was Theo with you at the time?'

Romy gulped, shaking her head. She wasn't supposed to say anything about Tania. And Aaron didn't seem to know anything about her being here.

'A hitch-hiker,' she came out with, thinking quickly. Well, wasn't that what they had both turned out to be that day? She cast a nervous tongue over her lips again. 'How—how did you find out, anyway?'

She took a step back as he moved nearer, and felt the unyielding solidity of the wall behind her.

'The garage thought fit to inform me,' he said. 'They did say a very pleasant young lady brought it in, but I think they were a little concerned that it might have been stolen.'

With no mention of Tania, she realised.

'Why didn't you tell me straight away what had happened?' He smirked, taking it better than she had imagined, she was more than relieved to discover, although his gaze was moving hotly over the slender lines of her body beneath the pink satin, causing heat to flood along her veins. 'What did you imagine I'd do...turn you over my knee and spank you?'

Feeling warm colour creeping up her throat into her cheeks, Romy wished she was a little more generously clad. She couldn't drag her eyes from that dark mat of hair in the V of his open shirt, stop herself breathing in the familiar, masculine scent of him.

'I expected at the very least to get a lecture about the incompetence of women drivers,' she admitted breathlessly, wanting to move away from him and finding that she couldn't.

'You really think of me as the ultimate male chauvinist, don't you?' he said on an exasperated sigh.

Romy tilted her head, the short, fair hair a pale cloud against her temples as she looked up into the dark, cleancut features. 'Aren't you?'

He smiled, an expression of wry humour. 'As a matter of fact, some of the most competent drivers I know are women . . . and some of the most capable people. Sandra for one.' He studied her obliquely, his eyes hardening. 'What's really eating you about me, Romy? The fact that I've broken through those impenetrable barriers you've set up against me . . . left you without any defences against those desires you want to deny and can't?'

'No!'

As she tried to move sideways, one stretch of his arm caught her, hauling her back, so that there was barely a hair's breadth between them. His chest was rising heavily, the tautness of his muscles apparent through the black, tailored shirt.

'What are you afraid of, Romy . . . this?'

Before she could stop him his mouth was swooping to take hers, his body forcing her back against the wall, its hard masculinity pressing into her softness, bringing an agony of want crushingly alive in her. Too drugged to resist, she strained towards him, wanting the possession of his mouth—his total domination of her body— hating herself, yet unable to avoid giving in to the primeval needs which racked her. His lips slid to her throat and she heard him groan as he breathed in the bathed sweetness of her skin, her willing breasts responding to the warmth of his hands through their flimsy covering. Self-respect urged her to fight him, and went unheeded to the point that a small cry of objection escaped her as he drew away.

The dark mask of his features was hard, his mouth tightly controlled, only the irregularity of his breathing hinting at the depth of passion he held leashed.

'The sooner you admit you want me, the sooner you'll be rid of those devils which are obviously giving that very complex little brain of yours hell. Get dressed,' he commanded—but softly. 'I want to take you out to dinner.'

'No...I don't want to go anywhere with you.'

She was trembling with need, and from the fear of the depth of her emotions for him. How could she tell him that what was giving her hell was the fact that she had fallen in love with him when he wasn't hers to love? She couldn't. She wanted to throw up at him about the house and how he had lied to her, but she couldn't do that either, not only because she was weary from fighting herself, but because if she told him she knew that he had bought this place he might guess that she had seen Tania, and she had promised her twin that she wouldn't tell.

Instead she said, hurt pride lending a flaying edge to her tongue, 'I've had enough of being a stand-in for the real thing.'

'So that's it,' he breathed, his broad shoulders sagging. 'Is that what this constant need to do battle with me is all about?' And when she couldn't look at him, her head averted, hiding the emotions she had to keep from him, she heard him say quietly, 'Why don't you stop living in your sister's shadow, Romy? Accept that a man can want you simply for yourself?'

She swung back to face him, her eyes angry. Who did he think he was, trying to psychoanalyse her?

'If you don't mind...I've got a headache,' she informed him pointedly. 'If it's all the same to you I intend to get an early night.'

'Such a convenient excuse.' Aaron's eyes glittered darkly, his mouth pulling down one side. 'It's one of your favourites for helping you out of tight spots, isn't it? So what am I supposed to do...just go?'

He looked so relentless that for a worried moment Romy wondered if he was going to ignore her very valid excuse and insist that she go out with him, and she breathed a small sigh of relief when she saw him moving towards the door. He turned as he reached it.

'The garage gave me to understand that you'd insisted on paying for the repairs to the car yourself——'

'That's right, and I will,' she interrupted, chin lifting, her lips tightening determinedly.

Anger flickered in Aaron's eyes—a dark flush spreading across his cheeks as his own mouth compressed.

'Like hell you will!' he expostulated, and stormed out, slamming the door hard after him.

She could have cried with frustration, and miserably she went into her bedroom, discarding her wrap to slip naked between the cool sheets. For a long time she lay there, listening to the interminable sound of the crickets—the eternal wash of the sea—her body burning for him, her heart aching for those tender words of love from a man whose interest in her, she knew, was only physical. And because she wouldn't jump into bed with him he had the audacity to suggest that she was living in her sister's shadow! The downright nerve of the man!

Angrily, she turned over, her gazed fixed abstractedly on the dim outline of the figurine on the dressing-table, until eventually her lids became heavy and she fell into a fitful sleep.

That night she dreamt that there were two of her—two halves of a whole that had somehow become separated—the one, an ordinary, indistinct figure chasing the other, an elusive, nymphlike creature in silk, across a deserted beach. First the pursued, then the pursuer, she saw the nymph hold out her arms to a man in black who caught her in his powerful embrace, but she *was* the nymph because she could feel his hands caressing her body through the gossamer silk—hear his deep, resonant voice murmuring her name as he laid her down on the sand. She cried in her sleep—tears of heart-singing joy. And then she was standing apart, looking down at the man and her other self—and he was making love to Tania.

CHAPTER EIGHT

ROMY woke with a start, blinking at the bright sunlight, her head muzzy, her mouth parched. Going into the bathroom, she gulped cold water thirstily from her cupped hand, loosely fastening the pink wrap she had slipped on, before wandering into the other bedroom.

'Tania?'

The bed was made up as if it hadn't been slept in, and trying to think clearly—her brain still foggy from the influence of her dream, Romy frowned. Surely Tania wasn't up already after being out late last night?

The front door was open, she noticed, when she came out of the bedroom, the fragrance of frangipani drifting in on the warm air, and Niki was dusting the ornaments on the hall table.

Smiling, she wished Romy 'good morning', and then they both turned, distracted by the sound of Aaron's Ferrari growling to an abrupt halt outside. He jumped out, taking the steps two at a time, and even without her glasses, Romy could make out his expression as his dark-suited figure came through the door, and she froze. There was a whiteness about the deep grooves around his mouth—every line of his clean-cut features taut from a barely restrained anger.

'All right, Niki . . . you can go.'

Unbelievably, Romy heard his curt dismissal of the other girl, and a surge of annoyance cut through her lethargy so that she was retaliating with, 'No! What right have you got, coming in here and ordering my sister's employees about?'

She noticed the puzzled look the servant girl gave her. Of course, Niki still thought *she* was Tania, she realised, exasperatedly. But, not wanting to be alone with Aaron

145

while he was in this mood, she was commanding, 'Stay here, Niki.'

The native girl looked anxiously from the man's hard features to Romy's flushed ones, but it was Aaron she obeyed, darting out of the door as soon as he stood aside for her to leave.

'She's *my* employee, my sweet,' he breathed, his tone anything but tender, his words a cruel reminder that he had recently bought this house. And probably Niki, too, she thought bitterly.

'No wonder you couldn't wait to get rid of me last night! Had you already planned this little escapade before I came down? Or were you so frustrated by my kisses you decided to call him afterwards?'

She didn't know what he was talking about, but his mood was frightening, and she jumped as he slammed a newspaper down hard on the hall table.

'Tania Morgan in a Suva nightclub last night with Government official, Danny Gower! Story by Quintin Swain!'

It was there in black and white—a picture of her sister and Danny splashed across the front page—and Aaron thought it was *her*!

He was moving slowly towards her—a vein pumping spasmodically in his temple—and her thudding heart was making her so weak she thought her legs would give way.

'You...you don't understand.' Nervously she changed her weight from one foot to the other, frightened by his inexorable expression.

'Then enlighten me, darling.'

Outside a bird whistled—then took off with a frenzied flapping of wings.

'It isn't me,' she breathed, her eyes appealing to the cold, amber ice of his, accepting now that it would be decidedly foolish to keep the promise she had made to her sister, so she uttered, desperate to convince him, 'It's Tania!'

She shuddered as he laughed harshly. 'And you expect me to believe that? Come on, sweetheart ... try again.'

'It is,' she stressed, panicking, smelling his anger mingled with the potent fresh scent of his cologne. 'She turned up yesterday when I was seeing Theo off... she came back with me...'

'Then where is she now?'

His tone was hard—disbelieving—and she threw back exasperatedly, 'I don't know!'

Fleetingly—concernedly—she wondered how her sister could have gone out with the other man—wondered if, in fact, she was still with him now. But Aaron's hands on her shoulders drove away all thoughts of Tania as he breathed heavily, his expression oddly pained, 'You'd rather be seen with a married man than admit you want me, wouldn't you? But I know that you've wanted me like crazy sometimes... last night being no exception. So did Danny satisfy those inadmissible urges, my sweet, or did you give him that same headache excuse you fobbed me off with?' And before she could answer, too outraged to speak he said thickly, 'Well, here's one occasion when you're going to have to come up with something better than that!'

'No!'

She fought him with all her strength as he scooped her up into his arms and started carrying her towards the bedroom, her robe falling open as she struggled in vain to try and stop him. She could feel the soft fabric of his suit against her flesh—arousing her in spite of herself—and as she beat at him harder with her fists— kicked out in panic with her flailing legs, he said grimly, 'Save your energy—you're going to need it.'

Her bed was still warm as he tossed her down on to it, pinning her there with the full length of his body. She gave a deep gasp, the weight of him against her causing pleasurable sensations to throb through her, producing a tight knot of need deep in her loins.

His hands were hard on her body, but they were only heightening her arousal, her breathing as ragged as his as he took her mouth in angry possession. He wanted to hurt her, and in a dizzy frenzy of desire she realised that she was glorying in his mastery of her, so that when his mouth found the aching fullness of her breast, she caught him to her, unable to fight him any more, her body craving his possession. Raw with longing, she felt her body's urgent response to the sweet torment of his mouth, the peaks of her breasts hardening as he tugged softly at each with his teeth, then encircled them with his tongue. Desire escalated, and she strained towards him, wanting him inside of her—to be part of him, her body racked with such an agony of wanting that a small, husky sob escaped her.

And then she was alone—bereft, a muffled protest leaving her lips with the dread that he had decided to abandon her. But he had only stood up to remove his own clothes, and, face flushed, her hair tousled against the pillow, she watched, half shyly, as he removed the last item, his body bronze—superbly muscular in its nakedness.

He rejoined her swiftly, drawing a throaty gasp from her as his hard body pressed hers into the mattress, the coarse hair of his chest tantalising against the softness of her breasts, his damp skin clinging sensuously to hers.

'I want you,' he groaned hoarsely, raining urgent kisses over her face and throat and breasts. He was tugging at the satin wrap so that compliantly she wriggled to make it easier for him to remove, her body arching instinctively towards his and the lips which were suddenly demanding full licence to every inch of her.

And then she was lost in a whirlpool of desire and sensation and want, her body softly perspiring—aching for the fulfilment he seemed bent on withholding from her—her small sob a desperate plea to him for release.

'Then tell me you want *me*!'

He was still angry with her—she could tell—and reluctantly she opened her eyes—saw him looking down at her, his features flushed, his own eyes glittering darkly with some intense, inner emotion she couldn't quite make out.

'Tell me you want me, Romy. Say it.'

She pressed her eyes tightly closed, her heart wrung by the anguish—the mysterious emotion in his voice—and suddenly she was crying, 'I want you! I want you! Oh God, I want you!' Her breathing was shallow, her heart thudding in anticipation as he lifted her hips.

And then he was inside her and she was moving with him, her body rising to meet his in a climax of mutual pleasure which had him groaning her name. She felt the convulsions of his body as he filled her with his soul, the muscles of his back taut beneath her hands. She gasped as her own desire peaked and then ebbed slowly away, leaving her so warm and fulfilled that, inexplicably, she found that she was crying—a flow of such intense emotion after the zenith of pleasure to which he had taken her, it couldn't release itself in any other way.

As if he understood, Aaron pulled her to him, holding her there for a long moment, and Romy pressed her lips into the hollow of his throat, liking the warmth and security his body offered, the musky scent of him, the slightly salty taste of his skin as she touched it with her tongue. When he moved on to his side, though, pinning her right arm awkwardly, she winced, suddenly made aware of the bruises she had sustained in the car.

'What is it?'

He was leaning above her, his eyes concerned, and she explained, love seeming to wrench her heart as he bent his head and very gently kissed her bruises.

'Did I hurt you?'

He'd said that once before, she remembered, when he hadn't intended to hurt her, but today he had, and she didn't know what to say. 'Yes, but I liked it'? He already knew that.

'It could easily have been worse,' she murmured, in an attempt to change the subject, because the sensual way he was looking up at her from beneath his dark lashes was sending desire spiralling through her again. 'We might both easily have been killed.'

'Your hitch-hiker?'

He said it as though he hadn't fully believed her story yesterday, and it occurred to her now that he might have suspected the person she was with to have been Danny Gower.

'No...Tania.' Her eyes clouded as she said it. She had forgotten Tania. 'I was telling you the truth earlier,' she murmured in anguish, seeing Aaron's incredulous expression. 'She was coming through Customs just as I was saying goodbye to Theo...'

'You mean...she really is back?' His brow furrowed as he raised himself up and stared at her. 'Then...that wasn't *your* photograph in the paper this morning?'

She couldn't understand how she could feel so numb after feeling so alive, the flush which touched Aaron's cheekbones leaving her speechless so that she could only nod, and her heart seemed to freeze when he dropped his head against the soft swell of her breast and groaned.

'Oh, God, why didn't you tell me?'

He was pulling her hard to him, and through her haze of bewilderment Romy's heart leaped as she realised that it was relief—not remorse—that had wrenched that sound from his throat, and that somehow—crazily!— he was glad that it was Tania with the other man and not her. She couldn't quite understand why.

'I shouldn't have made love to you like this...not in anger...' He broke off, lifting his dark head to scan her face, his eyes pained as they ran over the soft glow of her features—the suddenly avid sparkle in her own. 'Why didn't you say something to stop me?'

A warmth was spreading through her veins—a happiness so great she was almost afraid to think beyond it, and she smiled shyly. 'Were you listening to reason?'

He laughed softly—a self-condemnatory sound. 'No, I don't suppose I was.'

He was pushing her back against the pillow, feathering kisses over her face and neck, and she moaned softly, wondering how he could produce this ache of need in her again so soon after she had thought it fulfilled.

'All your efforts to convince the world that we were lovers seem pretty futile now, don't they?' she breathed, thinking of that photograph and wondering unhappily how her twin could have been so foolish as to see the other man again. She couldn't believe that her own sister could be behaving so promiscuously. After all, they'd both had the same reasonably strict and moral upbringing. 'I'm sorry.'

'Are you?' he asked, quietly, his eyes scanning her face as though he didn't quite believe her. 'I would have thought you'd be glad...after what I made you do under threat of telling Theo. I would have assumed you'd feel rather satisfied now...seeing the tables finally turned on me.'

Romy shook her head, but she couldn't think straight because the casual caress of his warm hands was making her long for him again. She didn't want him to know how much, but her breath was coming in short little gasps, and she saw him smile down at her—aware. Excitement rose in her as his caress suddenly turned erotic, and she twisted frenziedly against him as his mouth found her breast, his tongue teasing the hardening peak with consummate skill. His lips burned against her flesh, searing a line of kisses down her abdomen to the very core of her femininity and she gasped, desire holding her rigid, every nerve straining towards him for this ecstasy which she wanted to go on and on.

And the telephone suddenly shrilled beside the bed.

She tensed, and heard the small oath Aaron uttered before he reached over to answer it.

'Yes, all right, Niki. Put him on.'

Through her sensual lethargy Romy reasoned that the native girl must have gone up to the big house to join her fiancé when Aaron had sent her away, because she heard him say after a moment, 'Oh, lord! Yes, all right...I'll be up straight away.'

She couldn't look at him as he replaced the receiver, afraid that he'd read the disappointment in her eyes, but she couldn't help admiring the superb lines of his body as he slid off the bed, the sight of that broad, bronzed back, tight buttocks and long, muscular legs causing a familiar knot of longing in her stomach.

'There's some problem at the Lautoka plant, according to Richard Alison,' he told her, pulling on his clothes. 'Probably nothing that can't be sorted out easily enough...but I'm going to have to fly out there immediately. I'm sorry.'

He was tucking his shirt into his trousers—an entirely male action—and Romy was haunted by the thought of how many women he must have left like this—her own sister being one of them. She felt an inexplicable coldness surround her heart—a sudden tug of something remarkably like guilt. But what did she have to feel guilty about? she asked herself, rationally. Surely Tania couldn't care about him the way *she* did, when she could so easily go off with another man?

'I understand,' she responded, trying not to sound as uneasy as she was feeling.

And as if he could read her thoughts, he said, putting on his tie, 'I don't see why your sister's arrival here should make any difference to us.' He looked down at her where she lay with one arm lying flat across the sheet she had pulled up around her, the other in an arc above the shining cap of her hair. 'I want you to stay here...for us to continue...like this.'

The amber eyes held hers—dark with his desire for her—a look that made her body ache with need of him. He wanted her to stay here? But for how long? she wondered, and breathlessly, her heart racing, she voiced the question.

'That depends.' His voice was deep and warm, but emotionless—giving nothing away.

Romy swallowed, transfixed by that dark, sensual gaze. 'On what?' she breathed, her heart hammering.

He smiled, his hand, splayed against the narrow angle of his hips, strong, tanned hands which had driven her mindless for him, Romy thought, her stomach churning with fresh desire.

'On whether we start throwing things at each other.'
Half amused, his eyes were dark and probing—studying
her response. 'Or until our passion burns itself out.'

He wasn't committing himself, Romy realised. Nor did
she expect him to after so short an acquaintance.

'What about Tania?' she asked quietly, wondering with
some anxiety what her twin was going to say when she
knew. How did she really feel about him?

She saw him shrug—pick up his jacket off the bed.

'I can't think of any reason why she should object—
we weren't *that* involved,' he stated. 'But if it's bothering you at all...let me tell her.'

Clutching the sheet to her, Romy sat up, his words
sinking in. He and her twin hadn't been that involved!
A warmth suffused her cheeks. Could that be true?

'No...I'll do it,' she murmured, absently—dreamily.
After all, Tania *was* her sister. But between what Aaron
had just told her and the way Tania was behaving, surely
only her pride would be hurt, if anything, Romy mused,
solicitously. Surely her twin would understand...

'But won't other people think it odd...like Sandra?'
she queried, her eyes trained on his face, loving everything about it—the high sweep of that forehead, that
arrogant nose and that oh, so cruel mouth which was
curling with tenderness now.

'I don't give a damn what anyone thinks,' he said in
a low, sensual whisper, bending to rest his hands on the
bed so that his face was almost level with hers. 'After
that picture of Swain's, they'll probably deduce that
Tania's got herself a new playmate, but I don't mind
anyone knowing that I've fallen—hook, line and sinker—
for her beautiful sister.'

Fallen? In love? Her heart beat frantically. Was that
what he was saying...that he loved her?

Not in so many words, she realised, aching to hear
him say it.

His disparaging remark about her twin hurt, though
not as much as recognising that he seemed quite jus-
tified in making it. But his mouth was covering hers and

she gave a small moan, letting the sheet fall to twine her arms around his neck, kissing him back with all the intensity of her own love. Wanting him—needing him, she clung, but he pulled away, the frustrated sound which escaped him revealing just how much will power he had needed to exercise to do so.

'You temptress,' he whispered, his voice thick with desire. 'I'll see that you pay for that...later.'

His smile mocked, but it was a promise she knew he would keep, and a sensual warmth invaded her as he left and she heard him driving away.

Where would they go from here? Would the day come when Aaron would love her as much as she loved him?

She tried not to think that far ahead, hugging her new-found happiness to her. He'd said he wanted her to stay, but she couldn't do that indefinitely because of Fijian regulations on immigration. So how was he proposing to overcome that problem? By marrying her?

Her pulse quickened, and she told herself firmly that she was letting her dreams carry her too far. He hadn't mentioned marriage, she reminded herself, sitting up to look for her robe. He'd merely suggested that she stay until their passion burned itself out...

She didn't want to think about that either, too warmed by his caresses to ever imagine that it could, the only small cloud on her horizon—what Tania might say.

Seeing her robe on the floor where Aaron had tossed it, half dreamily she reached over to pick it up. And was stalled in the process as Tania called, 'Romy? Romy, I just saw Aaron driving out of here as I...'

She stopped dead in the doorway, her face turning ashen at the sight of Romy kneeling on the bed, trying to conceal her nudity with the pink wrap she was clutching to her.

'He made love to you.'

Tania's voice was barely a whisper, her wide, blue eyes hurt—disbelieving. She looked thin and frail in last night's clinging, black dress, the fresh, heavy make-up unable to hide the lack of natural colour in her cheeks, and Romy swallowed hard, a sick feeling washing over her.

'Tania, I can explain...'

'You don't have to.' Her tone was bitter. 'Everything's quite clear!'

There was no point in denying it, Romy realised disconcertedly, slipping into the robe. Her face was probably still flushed, her lips swollen from Aaron's kisses, and she knew there was a trace of his aftershave lotion still hanging on the air. Even so, Tania was taking it harder than Romy had imagined she would, especially in view of the fact that her twin was seeing another man.

'I didn't think you'd be this upset,' she began, finding her feet, but Tania cut in, her words biting and cruel.

'Didn't you?' Her eyes darted angrily from the rumpled bed to Romy's scantily clad figure. 'I come back and find my sister's been making it with *my* man, and you can't see why I'm upset!' Her voice was rising and bewilderedly, Romy could see that her twin was close to hysteria.

'I...he said that...' Half-way across the room, she paused, not sure what she was trying to say. Her sister was making her feel cheap, ashamed, and she couldn't see any reason why she should feel like that. 'He said that you weren't that involved,' she found the words to utter at last.

'Did he tell you *that*?' The acerbity in Tania's voice chilled Romy to the marrow. She stood rigid—immobilised—all traces of the joy she had known only minutes before flowing out of her. Had Aaron lied? She couldn't believe that he could have. And then a torturing little voice inside her head reminded her cruelly, he lied to you about the house.

Inwardly, she flinched, not wanting to admit it to herself. And she hadn't asked him about it earlier because she hadn't wanted to spoil the mood!

Angry, hurting inside, the flush was deepening across her cheekbones as she challenged hotly, 'If you think you love him so much, what were you doing with Danny

Gower last night?' And when Tania looked at her with hard, questioning eyes, Romy added, 'Your picture's in this morning's paper.' And with a catch in her voice, 'Aaron brought it down.'

'Oh, so you've seen that.' She strode into the room, dumping her bag rather unceremoniously down on to the dressing-table and knocking over the figurine. 'I've seen it already... but there's no truth in anything that's written there.' She flashed a glance at Romy. 'All right, I confess I went out with him a couple of times, but only for the odd, casual dinner... except that at a party last time I was a bit the worse for alcohol and I... well, I behaved rather stupidly...encouraging him, making him promises I had no intention of keeping, letting him kiss me in front of everyone. But I only did it because Aaron wasn't giving me enough attention.' There was a rebellious *moue* to her lips as she stared at herself in the mirror. 'As for last night, I met a friend, Sonya, and we went to a nightclub and saw Danny there quite by chance. I didn't want anything to do with him, but he came over, and I was in the process of telling him I wasn't interested any more when Quintin sprang from nowhere and got that picture. That's all there is to it, sister dear.' She dragged her gaze from her reflection to stare coldly at her twin. 'Satisfied?'

'No.' Romy met her gaze levelly, feeling numb and cold. She couldn't remember when she had last had real cross-words with Tania, and she wasn't enjoying it now. But driven by the nagging doubts that Aaron might not have been telling her the truth, she burst out, 'If it's all been so innocent between you and Danny, then where have you been all night?'

'With Sonya.' Tania's eyes widened, incredulously. 'God! You didn't think I'd spent the night with a man like that, did you? I told you yesterday that it was only a harmless flirtation, and it was true. I only wanted Aaron to *think* that I wanted another man. Perhaps that *was* stupid, but I've never been to bed with Danny and I've never had any intention of doing so. I'd never seriously involve myself in a relationship where someone else could get hurt. Despite what the papers say, Romy, I don't sleep with every man I go out with.' And bitingly, 'I would have thought my own sister would have credited me with more discrimination than that!'

Romy flushed, chastened—hating herself because she hadn't.

'Oh, I know I moaned about Aaron being too moral yesterday,' Tania went on, 'but I do like that in a man, believe it or not! I was just angry with him, that's all. And I didn't come home last night because when we left the club it was late, and Sonya's place was nearer, so it seemed the logical thing to stay with her.' Adding with cutting emphasis, 'Which is a lot more innocent than what you've been doing while I've been gone.'

Eyes glittering coldly, she turned away. 'When I asked you to come here, it wasn't only for my sake,' she was saying bitterly. 'I hoped that fresh scenery—a new environment—would help you get over Dad...bring you out of yourself...and it's certainly done that, hasn't it!' And with a sudden tremor, 'Aaron would have married me eventually...I know he would...if you hadn't come along and ruined it all!'

She had flung herself down on the bed—sobbing bitterly—and a sick, cold feeling spread through Romy's veins. It was years since she had seen Tania cry. She had always thought of her as the strong one, so confident and self-assured. But seeing her so helpless and vulnerable, a lump came up into Romy's throat. Suddenly, she was dropping down on to the bed beside Tania, cradling her sob-shaken body in her arms.

'I'm sorry,' she whispered, tears of remorse springing to her own eyes, because she had thought the worst about her twin; because she had hurt her so badly; because of Aaron. 'I didn't know you cared so much about him...'

She didn't know, either, how she could bear the pain—the hopelessness—that was seeping into her, reluctant to acknowledge the reason for it as she rocked her sister gently.

'He's the only man who's ever understood me,' Tania sobbed, her words muffled and broken. 'Dad didn't. Neither did any of those other fawning creeps who said they wanted to marry me. He's the only man I've every really respected . . .'

Yes, she could understand that, Romy thought numbly, breathing the perfume of her sister's sun-streaked hair. Aaron was the type of man you respected on sight. And last night he had told her to stop living in her sister's shadow—so perhaps she had been, she found herself half ready to accept, because she was only just realising something else, now: that she had been so blinded by Tania's success that she'd never even bothered to question whether or not her sister was really happy, and she knew now that she wasn't. She was even more insecure and lonely than Romy herself.

And suddenly she was accepting what that pain inside her was. A realisation that she could never trade her sister's happiness for her own. She had to go home. Get things into perspective again. The whole time she had been here she had been under a strain—from the pre-tence, the strong, physical attraction she had felt for Aaron, and then this love for him—and nothing had seemed real.

Who knew? Perhaps her love wasn't, she thought desolately, trying not to remember the feel of his lips on her body, the way he had held her when her emotion had released itself so uncontrollably after they had made love. But if it was, she decided in that moment—pain seeming to tear at her heart like cruel claws—then it was something that neither Aaron, nor Tania, were ever going to know about.

CHAPTER NINE

'You know...you've changed, Romy...since you've been away. Whatever happened to that strait-laced lady with long hair and glasses?'

Only just thirty, but with a crop of thick, silver hair, Roger Stainsbury was laughing at her, but in approval, Romy realised, as he stopped the car outside Henry Morgan's huge house.

'I really haven't a clue,' she joked, as the publisher escorted her to her front door, but there was an underlying sadness behind her laughter which the man was too shrewd not to notice.

'It's not only in appearance,' he commented, turning her to face him, although she knew she had surprised him three weeks ago when she'd burst into his office with her new book, her new hair-do, and the new degree of make-up she'd grown accustomed to wearing, enhancing the soft, island tan she'd acquired. 'You've changed in other ways, too. Become more confident—more self-assured.' And with a half-wistful smile, 'You met someone in Fiji, didn't you?'

She laughed again, uneasily, unable to meet those probing grey eyes. But she knew that what he was talking about was an over-all sophistication that had only come about because of her involvement with Aaron.

How could any woman emerge from the influence of that dynamic sexuality without acquiring *some*? she wondered wryly, pain twisting like a knife somewhere under her ribs. And if her friends and the men she met said she was beautiful now, it was only because he had convinced her that she was—because like some dark Svengali he had somehow brought her to life...

'Just one of those holiday romances,' she told Roger
lightly. Well, what else could she say? That every part
of her still ached with need for Aaron Blake? That often
she would wake at night and that need would be so great
that it took every ounce of her will-power not to sit down
and write to him? Roger would think she was crazy—as
she was beginning to herself.

The truth was that when she had left Fiji—getting an
unexpected cancellation on a flight out only hours after
Tania had come back and found her that morning—she
had been half hoping that Aaron might contact her. But
that had been nearly a month ago now and she still hadn't
heard from him. And though she had received several
chatty letters from Tania, they had made no mention of
Aaron. She wondered if they had got back together
again, knowing that she should have been happy for her
twin if they had. But she couldn't help the unimaginable
pain she was going through now in realising that she,
herself, had meant so little to him.

'I'm glad to hear that's all it was,' she heard Roger
say, though there was a note of scepticism in his voice.
'I'm expecting great things from you...and nothing
should be allowed to stand in the way of them.'

She gave him a weak smile. No, she wouldn't let him
down, she thought resolutely. When he had read her last
book he'd said it was the best thing she had ever written,
and now he had commissioned her to write two more in
the same vein. She couldn't tell him that that book had
been pure inspiration because she'd been in love. Writing
was her profession and she knew she was going to have
to get on with it, with or without Aaron. At least the
task ahead of her would help her to stop thinking about
him, she thought numbly.

'I'll be in touch,' said Roger, declining her offer of
coffee. But he did try to kiss her and she turned her head
in time so that his lips only brushed her cheek. He was
nice—gentle and reliable—and she wished she could have
fallen in love with someone like him. But she couldn't

get involved with anyone else yet, she told herself hopelessly—not while she still felt so deeply for Aaron.

She hardly heard the publisher's whispered 'goodnight', too preoccupied by the emotions which were
tearing at her, so overwhelmed by them that she didn't
realise that the hall light was on as she went inside, and
she started as someone appeared in the lounge doorway.

'Tania!'

'I've got that American job!' she enthused at once
with an expressive display of hands. 'It's only short-term
at the moment . . . six months or so . . . but I leave at the
end of the week and I had to see you before I left.' Smilingly, her gaze flicked over Romy's stylish white dress
with its red collar and belt. 'And we're wearing the same
colours again!'

So they were, Romy realised, already thinking how
exquisite her twin looked in the white, tailored jacket
and red, hip-hugging skirt. Pleased, too, to notice that
she looked more relaxed—far less strained—after her
holiday.

'That's great!' She felt a sudden rush of pride in her
sister's achievement. But she was having difficulty
coming to terms with the fact that Tania was actually
standing there when she'd believed her to still be in Fiji,
and the question was voicing itself before she could stop
it. 'What about Aaron?'

Her voice cracked slightly over his name, but her twin
didn't seem to notice, Romy realised gratefully.

Tania shrugged. 'We're through. We had a flaming
row over you the day you left and I only saw him once
socially after that.'

Romy looked at her, startled, and felt a queasiness in
her stomach—slightly breathless—as she remarked,
'Over me? But I thought that you and he . . .'

The other girl's eyes moved to the grandfather clock
which was just chiming eleven, the blue shadow on her
lids extending almost to the finely arched brows.

'We were never that involved... he was right when he told you that,' she admitted, somewhat sheepishly.

Romy stared at her, not quite believing what she was hearing.

Tania's eyes met the identical blue of her twin's. 'He never made me any promises... in fact, the relationship was totally one-sided. I think what I felt was a kind of hero-worship because he was the only man I've ever met who wouldn't let me have all my own way. And there was that physical thing, of course... that almost dangerous attraction he holds for the opposite sex.'

Romy's stomach tightened in a knot of intense anguish. She didn't want to remember.

'I think it was my pride more than anything else that day that made me so upset when I found out that he'd... been with you,' Tania stated, diplomatically, 'because as much as I adored him, we didn't have an awful lot in common. He'd rather have his head in a book or go out for a walk than throw a swinging party... and you know which I prefer. I think he'd probably have had more in common with you.'

Tania moved back into the lounge, Romy following her, her mind in a swim.

Aaron had told her the truth? That his relationship with her sister *hadn't* been serious? And they'd eventually split up because of *her*?

But that had been nearly a month ago and he hadn't bothered to get in touch, had he? she reminded herself bitterly, a sudden wall of sharp pain damming the hope flowing through her. Which could only mean that he hadn't really cared at all. So why had he wrung that response from her that day? she wondered wretchedly. Because of a need to satisfy his masculine ego? Had she been simply another conquest after he'd grown tired of her twin?

'There's one thing that's been worrying me for weeks,' she heard Tania saying and, looking at her, Romy noticed the anxiety in her twin's face—the concern in the blue eyes. 'Were you...that serious about Aaron?'

She felt the tears well up inside of her, but she fought them back. Tania would probably feel dreadful if she admitted that she had been, and she guessed it had already cost her twin a lot to confess to Aaron's casual disregard for her. So she forced a laugh—a shield against her very vulnerable emotions—to utter, 'Whatever gave you that idea? Of course I wasn't. So let's forget about him, shall we?'

Tania smiled, but there was a thin line still, between her brows.

'Well, if that little scene on the doorstep just now was anything to go by...I'd say you already had,' she said with a strained laugh, making Romy aware that her twin had seen her with Roger. 'I'm glad.' She put an arm affectionately around Romy's shoulders. 'I've felt awful for the past month...carrying on as I did that day. But if he didn't mean that much to you...' Her voice tailed off. Clearly she was relieved to drop the subject. As relieved as Romy was.

'Oh, and I've relinquished my tenancy, by the way.'

Romy looked at her incredulously. So all the strain— the pain she was suffering because of Aaron—had been for nothing?

'Why?' she asked, flabbergasted. 'You do mean the house in Fiji...'

Tania grimaced. 'All right, I know you've got a right to strangle me! But it will be enough having one home in Melbourne and another in New York for the next six months, without bringing Fiji into it as well!' She glanced round at the trunks and packing cases deposited at random around the large room. 'I see you've managed to sell this place, and from the look of things, you're moving out soon. Where are you going?'

Romy enlightened her. The trunks and furniture were going into store until the flat she was intending to buy became vacant, but she was having to move out of the house before then since she'd been offered a good cash offer for it—half of which would naturally go to Tania— and the purchaser was eager for immediate possession.

'I'll be staying in a small hotel for a few weeks,' Romy finished.

Tania looked aghast. 'Don't be ridiculous...that'll cost you a fortune!' And, as the thought occurred to her, 'Stay at my place!' she suggested readily. 'I shan't need it for...well...indefinitely, and it would be nice to think someone was looking after it, if only for a short time. You'd be doing me a favour, actually.' And with tears in her eyes, she was murmuring, 'I know we lead separate lives...don't see each other much these days, but gosh, sis, I'm going to miss you!'

And suddenly they were hugging each other and crying, her own flood of emotion, Romy realised guilt- ily, brought on by more than just her sister's going away.

But Tania's suggestion was a sensible one, and con- sequently, Romy moved into the penthouse apartment at the end of that week, knowing that she would be spoilt for anything else after the luxuriously spacious rooms and all the mod cons her twin had had installed. Some of the expensive ornaments around the place reminded her of those in the house in Fiji which saddened her, bringing back memories she didn't want. She was even more saddened when, unpacking a few of her own be- longings—the Hardy novels, her father's own books, and several ornaments which she treasured too much to put into store—she found that the wood carving she'd bought on the island had been damaged in the move and that the 'shadow' had almost completely broken away...

She worked hard throughout the following days, her writing more prolific than it had ever been; working, too, during the nights when she couldn't sleep, and there were plenty of those. And it was Aaron who dominated her thoughts in the dead of night when she lay in bed with her brain unoccupied—the way he smiled, his kiss, the hard thrust of his body as they'd shared that ultimate pleasure—until she was so feverish for him that the only way she could drive him from her mind was to get up and write.

Her work prospered, but her health was beginning to suffer, and lack of appetite, coupled with an inability to sleep properly, brought on bouts of dizziness and nausea. Even taking things a little easier for a few days didn't improve matters, until eventually she went to see her doctor, who confirmed what she hadn't, until then, wanted to accept.

She was pregnant.

She left the surgery that day with mixed feelings. Apprehension. Concern about the difficulties which lay ahead for a single mother and her child. And yet, deep down inside—a glimmer of pleasure and pride. She knew that if she could have chosen anything in this world to make her happy, it would have been Aaron's baby. But with him there, to protect and look after her. To share the joy and caring of their child with him...together. As it was, she was very much alone.

The next few days had her fighting an almost overwhelming urge to contact him—desperate for his support—but common sense alone kept her from doing so.

He hasn't bothered to contact you since you came back, a little voice inside continued to goad her, the truth of it piercing her heart like the point of cold steel. He could have telephoned, or dropped a line—however short—if she meant anything to him at all. But he hadn't, which was evidence in itself that she didn't.

Perhaps he was angry with you for walking out on him as you did, another little voice seemed determined to offer in his defence. After all, he *had* asked you to stay. And unwillingly, she remembered how remorseful he had looked when he'd said that he hadn't wanted to make love to her in anger. So perhaps he had thought she hadn't cared enough about him when he'd come back from Lautoka that day and found she had gone. Perhaps it was pride that kept him from contacting her...

But she didn't feel like making excuses for him, and under the warm spray of the shower she asked herself who she was fooling. He'd wanted a fling—a brief affair with her—that was all. Agonising to come to terms with, but fact, none the less. And if she had fallen in love with him and got herself pregnant because of it, who did she have to blame but herself?

Going into the bedroom to dress, she placed a gentle hand against her stomach. She wanted this baby—as much as it was possible to want anything. And she *would* cope, she assured herself for the umpteenth time as she pulled on her clothes. She was self-sufficient, wasn't she? So she would be able to provide a good home and education for her child. Perhaps not as comfortable a home as Aaron could provide, admittedly, but it would be a loving one, for all that. Only now she'd have to learn how to knit properly, she thought with a crooked smile, and reminded herself to put some more wool on her list before she went shopping.

Her errands that morning included a visit to the television studios. Tania had written to her from New York, asking if she would collect and forward a personal notebook which her twin had inadvertently left there, suggesting that if Romy went during the lunch-break and slipped through the back entrance, the chances were that she wouldn't meet anyone.

She didn't. Following Tania's directions, she found her office—fortunately the first one she came to—and went inside, grimacing at the thought of all the stringent security at the main entrance to the building when it was so easy to gain access from the rear.

But within seconds she had retrieved her twin's notebook from one of the shelves and was slipping out again, praying that she could get back to the car park without being seen. Since virtually everyone there knew that Tania had left to work in New York, she herself would have some explaining to do if she were, she thought, with a wry smile. Although the prospect of being acclaimed as Tania Morgan's twin wasn't as daunting as it had been, she discovered, hurrying past a cutting room and several temporary outbuildings. Somehow she felt she could cope with that now...

She started, transfixed, her breath catching painfully in her chest as the shadow of a familiar, dark figure fell across her path.

'Tania?' The amber eyes were studying her with a hard scrutiny—a deep line between the thick, black brows— and Romy's heart thudded. 'Or is it...'

He really didn't know, she realised, checking the convulsive little laugh which rose in her throat. The man she loved—whose child she was carrying—couldn't instantly recognise her from her twin! Well, of course he couldn't, she tried to tell herself rationally, particularly as she was just leaving the place where he must have thought Tania still worked. But it hurt—like hell.

'Oh come on, Aaron...surely you can tell?'

She hadn't intended to sound so curt, but it had suddenly struck her that he was *here*—where he thought Tania would be—and pain seemed to be eating her insides away, withering her control.

Beneath the silver-grey suit jacket, she saw the broad shoulders droop slightly, and a muscle played in the strong jaw.

'I called at the flat. I was hoping to find Romy there. Where is she?'

So he'd decided she was Tania! Dazedly, she tried to make some sense of what he had said and under the cool, red dress felt a surge of warmth wash up over her skin. He wanted to see *her*?

'I don't know.' It slipped out, and she didn't know why she had said it. It hadn't been her intention to mislead him, yet now she saw it as the only way of protecting herself against him until she found out exactly why he was looking for her. Behind her sunglasses she studied him with guarded eyes. 'Why did you think she was at my place?'

A breeze lifted the dark strands across his forehead, and Romy's throat constricted as she caught a waft of his cologne, so achingly familiar.

'I went to her old address and found she'd moved. The new owner seemed to think she was living with you.'

Because she'd told him that she was staying at her sister's, Romy remembered, dizzy from the violent hammering of her heart. She knew she would have to watch everything she said. Find out first what he wanted before she laid herself open to that dangerous masculinity—gave way to this overpowering impulse to tell him the truth. Because her feeling for him—this intense, burning agony of weeks—was screaming for release and, though she was finding this charade almost beyond her capabilities, she knew the only way she could conceal her love was to keep pretending to be her twin.

Blood pounded at her temples as she asked, cautiously, 'Why did you want to see her?' and her heart seemed to stop in anticipation of his reply.

He looked down at her, his eyes unfathomable, his face an expressionless mask against the rather weak blue of the sky.

'She left the island in rather a hurry. Since I had to come to Melbourne I was merely curious to find out why. And there's a small matter of a cheque for certain car repairs I wish to return to her.'

The autumn wind was chilling in itself but not anywhere near as much as the total indifference in Aaron's voice. So this was only a casual visit to him. A 'since I'm here, I may as well look you up' attitude. And he was still adamant about not letting her pay for the damage she had caused to his car, she realised distractedly, even thought she'd settled the bill with the garage herself that last day.

Pain creased her forehead and, determined not to let him see how his coldness tortured her, she gave a humourless little laugh.

'Of course... you don't like being walked out on, do you Aaron?' she remarked, her tone idle. And suddenly a sound made them both turn.

Someone had just come out of one of the temporary little outbuildings, and as the man started walking towards them, Romy tensed. If he showed any surprise at seeing Tania here, Aaron might well guess at the truth!

She bit her lip as the man drew level with them, but he merely uttered Tania's name with a curt nod and strode on, and Romy gave an imperceptible sigh of relief. She had to get away from here—from Aaron!

'Are you going to tell me where she is?'

Over her thoughts, his tone sounded almost threatening, his eyes raking over her. His stance was threatening, too. Hands on hips, legs planted firmly apart, his gaping jacket exposing the broad expanse of his chest which was rising sharply beneath the immaculate, white shirt, and for one frenzied moment she almost told him the truth.

'I told you...I don't know.' Panic crept into her voice, the way he was looking at her, so... feverishly, sending a host of dangerous sensations through her. 'She was with me for a while, but then one morning she just took off. I haven't a clue as to where.'

It was coming easily—to lie. And she was prepared to say—do—anything, just as long as he would go. She didn't think she could bear it much longer—being this close to him without being in his arms; not to be able to pour out her love and tell him that she was expecting his baby—feel the warmth and strength of his body comforting hers...

She brought her thoughts up quickly as she noticed the way he was studying her—his eyes darkening—before courtesy—at least, that was all she decided it was—forced him to ask, his tone almost bored, 'How was Romy?'

As if he cared!

She's pregnant. For one heart-stopping moment she thought she had spoken the words, a flush of scarlet tinting the skin across the high cheekbones. But if she told him now, he'd think he was hearing it from Tania.

Furtively, she darted a glance at him, wondering what he would do. Shoot back to the island as fast as he could and forget he'd ever set eyes on the Morgan twins? She didn't think so. Knowing him and that strong sense of propriety of his, he'd probably seek out Romy Morgan so that he could put a ring on her finger—make his child legitimate, she reflected cynically, and probably hate her for the rest of his life for trapping him into a marriage he didn't want. She shuddered, desperate that he should never find out. And anyone could come past at any minute! Someone who would remember that Tania was in America...

'She was remarkably well for not being involved with you,' Romy managed to say cuttingly through her fears and her intense need of him—the desolation inside. 'And now if you don't mind, I've got a lunch date.'

It wasn't the truth, although in her twin's case she knew it probably would have been, and despite all her instincts of self-survival which warned her she should be relieved to see him go, Romy's stomach was churning in sickening waves when she realised that he really was leaving.

'Still the same blasé female, aren't you, Tania?' His expression was deprecating, but she didn't care. Somehow she had managed to fool him, incredible though it was! Although she had wondered for a moment when he'd been looking at her so intently just now, and with immense relief she watched him walk away. But the feeling was short-lived.

Even before she had reached her car, she was hit by the agonising reality that she would probably never see him again and with half-paralysed limbs she clambered in and started the ignition, pulling the car blindly away

from the kerb. Her chest seemed to tighten as if it were
in a vice, and she was gasping for breath, the pain intensifying, rising up into her throat, emotion releasing
itself suddenly on one choking, soul-shattering sob. She
stopped the car abruptly—by some miracle, in a side
road—tears stinging her eyes which she couldn't fight
back, her slender body shaken by such devastating grief,
she wondered how she could ever come through it unscathed. But gradually she gained control of herself,
forcing back emotion so determinedly as she re-started
the engine, that it hurt.

When she let herself into the apartment, Avis, Tania's
cleaning lady was hoovering in the lounge, and quickly
Romy went through into the bathroom, not wanting Avis
to see that she had been crying.

She was in the bedroom, applying fresh make-up,
having decided that she had to get out, go for a long
walk—to the library, the museum, anywhere but stay
there and think about Aaron —when Avis put her head
round the door to announce that she was leaving.

'Thanks . . . for everything.' Somehow Romy managed
to sound cheerful, but her gratitude towards the plump,
elderly lady was genuine enough. It still didn't come as
a matter of course to let someone else do her chores.

'You look lovely, Miss Morgan,' the older woman
smiled, her breathing laborious in view of her weight.
'I don't know why you want to be a writer, I'm sure,'
she remarked, having been told, to her amazement, by
Tania several weeks ago, that the apartment was going
to be occupied by her twin. 'With those looks you could
have made it in television the same as your sister
has . . . still could.'

Romy blushed and gave a dismissive little laugh,
knowing that she could never explain to Avis how much
fulfilment she found in her own work.

'I prefer the quiet life,' she responded candidly, relieved that the cleaner hadn't seemed to notice any signs
of her tears. So much for clever make-up! she thought

wryly. At least the charade in Fiji hadn't been entirely
for nothing.

Moments later she heard Avis call 'goodbye' and
thought she heard her mumble something else. But then
the front door closed and everything was quiet.

With a last glance at her reflection to check that she
looked presentable enough for the outside world, Romy
went into the lounge. And gasped, the colour draining
out of her cheeks at the sight of the man sitting in an
easy chair, looking for all the world as if he belonged
there.

'H-how did you get in?' she stammered, after what
seemed an endless moment.

Aaron's lips curled in amusement—in perfect cogni-
sance of her disorientation. 'Your cleaning lady. I came
up just as she was coming out. I simply told her Miss
Morgan was expecting me, so she allowed me access.'

The colour was returning to the fine-boned cheeks,
but her legs felt like jelly.

'I told you . . . Romy isn't here.' Her voice shook and
she swallowed hard. Tania wouldn't falter. Or would she,
Romy wondered, in the face of that indomitable
masculinity?

Her nails dug into her palms as he stood up and came
slowly towards her, his movements easy—self-assured,
his presence dominating even in the spacious luxury of
the penthouse.

'I know.' The cruel mouth curved in a smile which
didn't touch his eyes. 'I came back to see *you*.'

'Why?' It was a hasty, breathless response as she
looked at him uncertainly, silently querying his motives.
God knew! she had asked for this. But was he so convinced she was Tania that he had come back to . . . to
what? She hardly dared to imagine.

His hands came to rest on the back of his hips as he
studied her, his gaze raking over the blonde bob, the
over-bright eyes and tantalisingly full mouth, before
moving down over the simple scarlet dress with its hip-

hugging belt, to the matching high-heeled sandals she wore, and something tugged at his lips.

'Why do you almost invariably wear red?' His smile was cynical beneath the equally cynical lift of a thick eyebrow. 'Is it symbolic of a subconscious desire to court danger?'

She wasn't sure what he was driving at, but the sensual undertone in his voice made her pulse quicken—threatened her defences. But he was talking to Tania, she reminded herself brutally, lifting her small chin in painful challenge, her eyes glitteringly clear.

'What do you want?'

His gaze locked with hers for a long moment—one breath-catching moment when she mistook something in those amber eyes for tenderness as he said softly, 'You.'

Romy felt as if she had been knifed. She couldn't stay here and take this, feeling like an eavesdropper on something she didn't want to hear and, hurting unbelievably inside as she was, it took all the dignity she could muster to say coolly, 'Well, that's just too bad, Aaron, because as I told you earlier... I've got a lunch date.'

Which must surely have him wondering why she had come back here, she thought, realising that she was in danger of tripping herself up with her own lies, and as she made to brush past him she felt a grip like iron on her lower arm.

'Break it.'

Pulse thumping, every nerve leaping into traitorous life at his touch, somehow she managed to meet his gaze levelly to demand, 'Why? What right have you got coming in here ordering me about?'

His face was devoid of expression as he scrutinised her, but she noted the deep lines around his mouth—the dark smudges beneath his eyes that she hadn't noticed before.

'We parted on rather bad terms just now... and on the island. But it seems a pity to throw away what we once had when we could both enjoy a very...pleasing relationship.'

She couldn't believe she was hearing this. He had come here initially looking for *her*, Romy, and it didn't matter at all to him that he hadn't found her. Obviously where he was concerned, one twin was pretty much the same as the other!

A lump in her throat seemed to be choking her and, wondering how he would answer, she bit out in a voice tremulous with accusation, 'You made love to Romy.'

His hand dropped away from her and he exhaled deeply, his chest muscles flexing beneath the fine shirt.

'She made it clear from the outset that she wanted me to,' he answered, his voice dispassionate, yet low, as though for some reason he were having a job keeping it under control. 'What man can be blamed for finally giving in to a temptation like that?'

Pain urged her to hit out at him—to claw her nails down that arrogantly handsome face of his—and only pride stopped her. He'd know then, wouldn't he? she realised, her face taut with anguish.

'And you're suggesting that *we* should be lovers again?' It was an effort keeping up this cool, Tania-like attitude when every trembling nerve in her body was threatening to betray her—to bring about her total collapse. 'Well, I'm sorry, but you really don't do anything for me any more, Aaron Blake,' she succeeded in getting out in a desperate attempt to make him go. 'So I'm afraid you and I are through.'

She had underestimated him if she had thought that he would take that for an answer, and she gave a small shocked cry of protest as he reached for her, pulling her to him.

In a daze of blind anger and panic she heard his, 'Well, let's see, shall we?' The words were husky and torn from him. And then she was fighting him, struggling frantically to avoid his mouth which was suddenly capturing hers with ruthless determination. She was drowning in the scent of him—in a sea of treacherous desire, feeling the warmth of his fingers in her hair as they imprisoned her against him, his other arm, like a steel band around her middle, making her vibrantly alive to the hard masculinity of his body.

She made a small guttural sound as he tipped her head back to allow his kiss to deepen, and the coaxing intimacy of his tongue seemed to snap her last shred of control. With an abandon she was already despising herself for, she slid her arms up around his neck to clutch him to her, kissing him back with a desperation that drew a deep groan from his throat.

As he drew away, reason surfaced, and on such a wave of self-loathing that she couldn't look at him, her lids pressed tightly against the hot tears of frustration and anger which were suddenly burning behind them.

'Open your eyes... Romy.'

His deep, unexpected murmur of her name jolted her into obeying. Shocked, she stared up at him with moist, startled eyes. Thought that he looked as pained as she felt.

'Why?' he asked quietly, a deep line between his brows.

Shaken from his kiss, and the shock of being found out, Romy couldn't answer, the only thought in her mind that her response to that kiss must have given her away.

A dark flush was tinging the skin across Aaron's cheekbones as he said, impatiently, 'Why did you pretend to be your sister? Would you really have let me walk away again still thinking you were Tania... knowing I probably wouldn't be back?'

Romy frowned, unable to make any sense of what he was saying—of why he sounded so angry. But if he had a right to be angry, she thought bitterly. Well, so did she!

'I didn't think it mattered to you which twin you hopped into bed with,' she flung at him, her eyes two bright sparks of hurt fury. 'A moment ago when you thought you were seducing Tania...'

'Stop it!'

She winced as he caught her roughly by the arms, his eyes so wild and . . . hurt? she thought, puzzlingly, that she couldn't meet their stormy, amber depths.

'You stupid little idiot!' Aaron rasped between breaths. 'Did you really think I fell for that ridiculous bit of play-acting?'

Accusation was still paramount in Romy's eyes as she swung to face him.

'Oh, I'll admit you had me fooled for a few minutes when I saw you outside the studios,' he assured her with a humourless smile. 'But we've been there before, darling . . . remember?'

She didn't want to, memories of the time she had spent with him on the island stirring feelings she didn't want to feel.

'Oh, you put up a pretty good show,' he acknowledged brittly, 'but I do know the differences between you. The way you stick out your chin when you want to challenge something I've said.' And with a grimace, 'Which you do most of the time, incidentally. The way you blush more easily. But even without that there's one glaring error you made as your twin . . . one you're still making, sweetheart . . . and that's that Tania and I have never been lovers.'

Romy stared at him, her lips parted in disbelief.

'But I thought . . .'

At that moment she was too nonplussed to think anything, and dazedly she heard him say, 'Oh, I won't pretend that the temptation wasn't there.' A smile played around the corners of his mouth. 'After all, she looks exactly like you. But she wanted more than a physical relationship, which I couldn't give her. She knew that all along. And between her not being prepared to settle for anything less than a wedding ring, and my having absolutely no designs on getting married, we really didn't amount to much. But with you . . .' His eyes were dark with desire, and something else she couldn't make out as they raked over her face and throat—the smooth lines of her shoulders beneath the red dress—and little *frissons* of awareness shivered through her. 'Every time I kissed you, you virtually had me losing control. Tania never had that effect on me. That's why it didn't take me long to realise it was you when I saw you earlier...because it was there almost instantly...that desire to take you in my arms and hold you...make love to you, right then and there in that car park. I need you that much.'

Romy's heart swelled—emotion flooding her—but she held herself rigid, considering his words.

Need, not love, a little voice inside her warned, because she was dangerously close to accepting him on whatever terms he laid down. And she had already shown him that she, unlike Tania, would settle for less than marriage...

She looked at him obliquely, her lashes concealing the pained emotion in her eyes. 'If you knew...why did you leave?'

He grimaced. 'You didn't seem over-keen that I should stay. There's a limit to how many rebuffs a man can take, my love. But when I was driving around afterwards I thought that perhaps you were pretending to be Tania to protect yourself from me, so I took the chance that you'd come back here and came after you, since I'd decided that you'd only be needing protection if you were afraid of me...or...yourself.' His tone had become sensuously soft, his eyes, like pools of dark, gold sherry as they probed the anguished blue of hers. 'And that could only mean that you care about me a lot more than you want to admit...doesn't it, Romy?'

He didn't need to ask. She had confirmed it indelibly in that one kiss. And as he drew her nearer, she wanted to submit. To throw her arms around his neck and cry out that she did care about him—very much. That she loved him with all the depth and strength of her being and the proof of the child growing inside her. But she held back, hurting too much as she remembered his casual indifference earlier.

'You didn't seem to care too much whether you found me or not,' she demurred, her palms flat against his chest—holding him away—and beneath her fingers she felt the heavy thunder of his heart. 'It doesn't do much for a girl's ego to know she's being looked up just because you happen to be here,' she went on, adding with an injured little pout, 'and you didn't try to contact me before.'

Sunlight was streaming in through the panoramic windows, making his bitter-chocolate hair shine like wildfire, and Romy had to restrain a sudden urge to run her fingers through the dark strands.

'All right . . . perhaps I should have,' Aaron was admitting with a heavy sigh. 'But it does work both ways, you know, Romy. No man likes to be left flat the way you left me. When I came back that night, I didn't know what the hell had happened to you, and all Tania said was that you'd had enough of the island and had decided to leave.'

Which was precisely what she had told her twin, Romy reflected.

'All I could assume was that you'd regretted what had happened between us afterwards,' Aaron was continuing. 'I thought you probably hated me because of what I'd done . . . because I damn near raped you that day, thinking it was you with Danny Gower. And thinking how you must have felt and despising myself for the way I'd behaved, I couldn't bring myself to come here or even telephone.'

There was a strange inflexion in his voice as he finished speaking, and suddenly the dark smudges beneath his eyes looked darker, the grooves around his mouth deeper—making him look tired—almost ill. Still attractive, Romy thought, but not quite the thrusting tower of strength and sheer male arrogance she had encountered on their first meeting. She couldn't understand this change in him.

'I don't hate you,' she whispered, her thoughts a maze of confusion. 'I left because ... because I thought I'd be coming between you and Tania if I stayed.'

'But I told you that last day that we weren't involved.' He was shaking his head, his brow furrowing deeply. 'Why didn't you believe me?' he asked, hoarsely.

She couldn't tell him that her twin had led her to believe otherwise. Anyway, she could forgive Tania that now. She could understand why her sister had been so besotted, and upset at the thought of losing him. That dark sexuality of his could ensnare any woman—even without love. Hadn't she been a victim of it herself from the very beginning—even before her feelings had intensified and grown?

'You hadn't exactly been truthful with me about everything else, had you?' she accused softly, her fingers running absently over the silver-grey tie. 'You let me believe Theo still owned the house, when, in fact, you'd bought it yourself *and* waived the three-month restriction,' she reminded him, remembering what Tania had told her when she had arrived on the island that day. 'So you had no real threat with which to hold me to our bargain ...'

She stopped short, swaying unsteadily as waves of nausea and dizziness swept over her.

'Are you all right?' Aaron's deep voice was strung with concern, but the arm going around her waist seemed to put new life back into her.

'I-I think so,' she breathed, her hand to her mouth, and she was suddenly very much aware of his puzzling examination of her.

Of course, he didn't know that there had been repercussions from their lovemaking that day. And he mustn't know, she told herself, fiercely, fear that he might insist on a wedding when he'd already said he had no designs

on getting married, making her stomach clench
sickeningly.

'Why did you lie to me?' she said woundedly, fighting
back the nausea. 'Insist we pretend to be lovers if Tania
and you weren't that involved? To protect her reputation? Or was it to protect Danny's family because...because of what happened to...' tentatively,
she dropped her gaze, fixing it on one of his shirt buttons
'...to your mother?'

The broad chest expanded deeply. 'You still don't understand, do you?' he exhaled, and Romy met his dark
gaze with a query in her own. 'Do you really think I've
got such a deep-rooted psychological problem that I'd
go to those lengths just to save another man's marriage?' He laughed harshly. 'I'm surprised you didn't
also imagine I was so sick with jealousy over Tania and
Gower that I was using you just to boost my own ego.'

Romy blushed scarlet. Well, hadn't she? she thought,
sheepishly. Although she wasn't going to admit that to
Aaron.

'Oh, I agree that I saw my taking you to that party
that night as a way of showing Swain that your sister
wasn't a subject for any more scandal. And yes, I _was_
a little concerned about a family being split, but not to
the point of being obsessive about it...exploiting you
because of it. Helen Gower's strong enough to take care
of herself—and foolish enough to forgive her husband's
infidelities, so I imagine she'll stick with him to the bitter
end. Incidentally,' he added, 'Tania explained to me why
she behaved as she had with Gower...said she'd told
you, too, that they weren't having an affair, and I'm
glad. She's too intelligent a girl to ruin her life with a
man like that,' he commented, and happily, for the first
time, Romy detected an indulgence—a softening in him—
towards her twin.

'Still, I would have thought it would have been obvious to you by now,' he went on, 'that why I insisted
you keep up the pretence...go everywhere I wanted to

take you *and* as your lover...was for the pure and simple reason that I wanted you in my arms. Oh, yes,' he said softly, with a self-censuring smile, when he saw the incredulity in her eyes, 'you knocked me sideways right from that first day. I couldn't understand it because I thought you were Tania, and I'd never wanted her quite like that before. Then, when I realised the truth...'

He was drawing her gently towards him, making her pulses leap as he smiled down at her with darkly hypnotic eyes, and she remembered wondering why her twin hadn't said more about him in the beginning—boasted of her involvement with him—however slight. And now she knew why. Tania had had her pride. And Aaron had been one man she couldn't bring to his knees—unlike all the other men she'd dated. She'd used that very expression herself at the airport that day, Romy ruminated, realising now that although her sister hadn't denied the suggestion that day that she and Aaron were lovers, she hadn't then, or at any time, actually admitted to it, either. And now that Aaron had told her quite frankly that they weren't—never had been—somehow Romy knew that he was telling the truth.

'You were like a frightened bird,' he breathed softly into the pale gold of her hair. 'Frightened of me...and of this explosive sexual chemistry between us. And if I'd told you the truth...let you know I had no hold over you—and God knows, I wanted to!—you would have flown...and I'd never have seen you again. My buying the house was only a last-minute decision anyway,' he told her, 'since Theo was so keen to be rid of the responsibility of it. As it was on my land it seemed the most natural thing to do, and negotiations were still being finalised when you arrived.' He pulled a wry face. 'I had quite a job persuading Theo not to say anything to you. As he thought you were Tania he couldn't understand why you shouldn't know, and I could hardly tell him that I wanted his silence to keep you around for...personal reasons. At some stage, I'm going to have to do a bit of explaining to him.'

'You're devious!' she hissed, but breathlessly, because the warmth of his nearness and that familiar, spicy scent of him were making her senses swim.

'Yes,' he acknowledged softly, his arms tightening around her. 'And for your information, dearest, I didn't just *happen* to be in Melbourne today, although I had to hang on to some pride when you seemed so determined to avoid me earlier. But really...' And his voice had grown ever softer—deep and warm and tender. '...I came here solely with the intention of finding you, darling. I love you, Romy.'

The words seemed wrenched from him and, incredulously, she stared up at him, her lips parted and trembling. Colour was creeping up her throat into the fine-boned cheeks and through a rush of dizzy emotion she tried to say something—felt the giddiness coming over her so swiftly that she couldn't. And the next thing she knew she was lying down in Tania's luxurious bedroom and Aaron was sitting on the edge of the bed, leaning over her.

When she glanced up at him with a feeble, 'I'm sorry,' relief seemed to soften the strong angles of his face.

'I've never told a woman I love her before,' he said gently, smiling, 'and that wasn't quite the reaction I was expecting when I did. What is it, Romy?' Suddenly his voice was thick with anguish, and the eyes which scanned the delicate, pinched features were dark with concern. 'You're ill...'

His fingers were gently stroking her temple, and he looked so pained that she reached up and touched the strong line of his cheek, her face pale against the creamy satin of the pillow. He loved her! Then she hadn't dreamed that!

'Of course I'm not, you idiot,' she smiled tremulously, her fingers making a tentative trail down his jawline to the warm, throbbing pulse in his throat. And she knew she could tell him now. 'I'm going to have your baby, that's all.'

Astonishment etched the strong features to be chased away by... pleasure, she realised, with an insurmountable rush of joy. And then he was gathering her to him, holding her so tightly that it hurt.

'Oh, darling... why didn't you tell me straight away?' His voice was husky—agonised—his lips against the softness of her hair—and when he eventually lifted his head and looked at her, she noticed, with a tug of heart-rending emotion, that his cheeks were wet. 'Did you think I wouldn't want it... *you*?'

Seeing him so moved brought a lump to Romy's throat and she nodded, swallowing. 'We didn't plan this... I mean, I didn't even know if you liked children, or if you'd be angry...'

'Angry? Oh God, you little fool!' He was crushing her to him again, holding her as if he didn't ever want to let her go, the hard, male strength of him making her feel wonderfully secure—warm and safe. 'I wants lots of children... a happy family. Love... security... all those things I've never had myself. But first,' he said, positively, 'I want you. I want you to come back to Fiji with me now... today. And we'll be married as soon as possible...'

He stopped short, obviously realising how presumptuous he was being.

'You do want that, don't you?' he asked cautiously, frowning. 'You do love me?'

Romy laughed at the uncertainty in his face, her arms going around his neck. 'Of course I do,' she breathed exuberantly, to both his questions, a warmth singing through her veins as he pushed her back against the pillow. He would look after her—protect her, be there to see her body grow ripe with his seed. And she would give in return, through the years ahead, all the love he had missed in his own life... but she couldn't think too deeply at that moment because his hands had found the buttons of her dress and, moving inside, were producing that familiar, exquisite pleasure in her—and with such infinite tenderness as they found the creamy swell of her breast that she gave a soft moan.

Her eyes slumbrous with desire, she smiled coyly up at him and felt a sensual little flutter in her stomach as she met the warm desire in his response. She reached up, drawing his head down to the dark, tumescent peak of her breast, the moist warmth of his mouth bringing a small sound to her lips—a little murmur of wanting.

'Not here,' he whispered, his breath fanning the pale gold of her skin. 'This has to be *our* bed this time—in *our* home. 'I've no intention of making love to you in Tania's bed.'

She'd forgotten how moral he was and, with a cursory glance over the luxurious bedroom with its satin drapes, plush carpet and exclusively feminine fittings, she had to admit that for them to make love in here would be rather unethical. After all, Tania had loved him, too, in her own way. But at that moment Romy wanted him too much to care.

'That didn't stop you last time.' There was a soft plea in her reminder.

'That was different. I was angry with you...' His answer produced a deep ache in her loins, intensifying as he continued feathering kisses across the pale skin of her breast. 'I'd already been sick with worry the night before when I found out you'd had that accident with the car. I almost told you then how I felt about you, but you seemed so hostile towards me...'

'Because Tania had arrived and I thought you wouldn't want me when you knew,' Romy admitted shyly, her eyes closed against the sweet torment of his lips which had somehow found their way to her midriff.

'And because of it I thought you didn't care...' She heard him groan deeply. 'When I saw that photograph in the paper and thought I'd lost you to Gower...I'm afraid that was the end of my control.'

'I'm glad,' she whispered raggedly, because the memory of his hard possession of her that day, coupled with the sensation of his lips tracing light kisses over her stomach—his infinite gentleness now—was making her crave his total dominance like one demented. Mindlessly she caught at his sleeve, her urgent fingers twisting in the fabric to try and pull him down on to her, her plea a small sob.

'What about this lunch date?' It was a tender admonishment as he slid up the bed towards her, his face flushed with desire, a need for reassurance in his eyes. 'Don't you think he'll mind being stood up?'

Romy smiled at the little line of doubt between the dark eyebrows. 'Purely fictitious,' she breathed in admission, and gave a little groan of disappointment as he suddenly got to his feet and lifted her up into his arms.

'I said I wouldn't make love to you in Tania's bed,' he reminded her firmly, carrying her out of the room. 'And I'm not going to.' And with a crooked twist to his lips he strode across the apartment, his tone sending a drugging warmth tingling through her as he murmured with rigid purpose, 'But I've certainly got no adverse feelings about using her spare room.'

The sunset was making the horizon burn like a crimson flame, its path of fire spreading over the blue water and the white beach so that they gleamed sapphire and gold, the vibrant colour reaching up over the sturdy palms and the huge, white house to the bougainvillaea beyond the terrace, and Romy stood, hugging a secret to her.

It had been a perfect day all round. She had seen the doctor, who had confirmed that the unborn baby was developing normally, and she'd had a letter from Tania, too. It stated, as all her twin's frequent correspondence did, that she was enjoying hosting the latest TV breakfast show in New York. But she could be staying much longer than anticipated, she'd informed Romy, because she'd fallen for a lighting technician—'of all things!'—and was certain that this time it was the real thing.

'Peter's quiet and unassuming...but he keeps me in line,' Tania had written, adding with a blatant honesty, 'which is what I need!'

Romy smiled to herself, as happily surprised by her sister's news as Tania had been when Romy had written and told her about her own marriage to Aaron and her pregnancy, and suddenly she caught her breath, her heart missing a beat as she heard that familiar stride on the stones behind her.

She turned, and with one determined movement from him she was in his arms again and he was kissing her madly—passionately, because they'd been apart for at least five hours.

It had been like this for the past three months, Romy reflected, blissfully, nuzzling against the broad width of her husband's shoulder—drowning in the fresh, clean scent of him. Three happy months when they couldn't get enough of each other; when their urgent need of one another had him sweeping her up into his arms and carrying her upstairs as soon as he came home—much to the silent understanding of the newly wedded Niki and Raku. But tonight, Romy realised, Aaron had a lot of questions to ask first.

'Did Chisholm say everything was all right? Are you taking things as easily as you should? You've got something to tell me, haven't you?'

God, he could read her mind like a book!

'Everything's perfect.' Laughingly, she reached up and touched his rough cheek, the concern in his face tugging at her heart. And a little *frisson* of desire leaped through her as he responded by lifting her up into his strong arms.

'In that case, do you think my little heir would mind if I make love to you?'

Romy gave a soft moan of approval, her arms going around his neck, and in mock admonishment she—

queried, smilingly, 'Heir? You're determined it's going to be a boy, aren't you?'

Aaron stood still, looking down at her, the flame that scorched the horizon turning his hair to fire—mirroring the love and tenderness in his eyes.

'Boy...girl...I'll love it just as much—whatever it is,' he whispered into the soft, silken bob. 'Though I can't promise that I'll ever love anyone else as much as I love you. Do you think it will mind?'

His voice was deep—ragged with emotion—and Romy clutched him to her, her heart overflowing with her own love.

'I don't think so,' she murmured, immersed in this perfect happiness—the joy such as she could never have imagined in being Mrs Aaron Blake. 'But there's just one thing...' She laughed up at him again as he was carrying her inside, and breathed, with a triumphant gleam in her eyes, *It's* twins!'

Harlequin Presents

Coming Next Month

1079 DARK DESIRING Jacqui Baird
Believing her trip to Sicily with her boss is for business, Helen finds
herself trapped. Carlo Manzitti, the Italian who captured Helen's heart
two years before, and from whom she had fled, has arranged the whole
thing. This time he intends to keep her.

1080 THE POSITIVE APPROACH Emma Darcy
Ben arrives in Sarah's life like a rescuing knight, with a solution to both
their problems. He needs a wife; Sarah needs a fresh start. He says he'll
make all her dreams come true—but eventually Sarah begins to want
more than just dreams....

1081 ECHO OF PASSION Charlotte Lamb
Zoe, hurt by Rory Ormond before, is determined to prevent the same
thing happening to another young girl. She believes she's over their affair
and strong enough to thwart Rory's plans without danger to her own
emotions. Until she meets Rory again.

1082 LOVESCENES Sandra Marton
Shannon angrily voices her opinion on music celebrities who walk into
jobs for which real actors would give their eye teeth. Unfortunately,
Cade Morgan hears her—and can't resist the challenge. That's how it all
starts....

1083 WISH FOR THE MOON Carole Mortimer
Lise Morrison was an innocent trusting girl until her love for Quinn Taylor
shattered her world. But Elizabeth Farnham is less vulnerable, now, more
sophisticated. She can cope with anything...except perhaps the
reappearance of Quinn.

1084 TIME OUT OF MIND Kay Thorpe
Adria Morris, suffering from amnesia, is startled when Kyle Hamilton
appears and proves she is his late brother's wife. Even after her return to
their family home on St. Amelia, her amnesia persists. Adria must decide
whether to marry Kyle, or leave behind all hope of regaining her memory.

1085 LOST LAGOON Anne Weale
Interior designer Alexandra, headed for the top, isn't going to be swayed
from her career, even by someone as special as Laurier Tait. And Laurier
isn't the type to settle for a brief autumn affair—he wants a full-time
partner in life.

1086 THE ORTIGA MARRIAGE Patricia Wilson
Meriel has made a life of her own since her stepbrother, Ramon Ortiga,
rejected her love. Now, because of her young half brother, Manuel, she
returns to the remote Venezuelan ranch to find Ramon as arrogant as
ever—and her attraction to him still as strong.

Available in June wherever paperback books are sold, or through
Harlequin Reader Service:

In the U.S.
901 Fuhrmann Blvd.
P.O. Box 1397
Buffalo, N.Y. 14240-1397

In Canada
P.O. Box 603
Fort Erie, Ontario
L2A 5X3

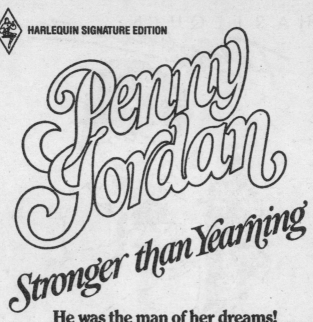

Penny Jordan

Stronger than Yearning

He was the man of her dreams!

The same dark hair, the same mocking eyes; it was as if the Regency rake of the portrait, the seducer of Jenna's dream, had come to life. Jenna, believing the last of the Deverils dead, was determined to buy the great old Yorkshire Hall—to claim it for her daughter, Lucy, and put to rest some of the painful memories of Lucy's birth. She had no way of knowing that a direct descendant of the black sheep Deveril even existed—or that James Allingham and his own powerful yearnings would disrupt her plan entirely.

Penny Jordan's first Harlequin Signature Edition *Love's Choices* was an outstanding success. Penny Jordan has written more than 40 best-selling titles—more than 4 million copies sold.

Now, be sure to buy her latest bestseller, *Stronger Than Yearning*. Available wherever paperbacks are sold—in June.

STRONG-1R